# MOUNTAINS
# MEMORIES &
# *Mistletoe*

# MOUNTAINS MEMORIES & *Mistletoe*

*Romance Makes Coming Home*
*Adventurous in Two Christmas Novellas*

## JANET LEE BARTON
## KATHLEEN MILLER

BARBOUR
PUBLISHING

© 2006 *Making Memories* by Janet Lee Barton
© 2006 *Dreaming of a White Christmas* by Kathleen Miller

ISBN 1-59789-340-4

All scripture quotations are taken from the King James Version of the Bible.

This book is a work of fiction. Names, characters, places, and incidents are either products of the author's imagination or used fictitiously. Any similarity to actual people, organizations, and/or events is purely coincidental.

Cover image by John Kelly/Iconica

Published by Barbour Publishing, Inc., P.O. Box 719, Uhrichsville, Ohio 44683, www.barbourbooks.com

*Our mission is to publish and distribute inspirational products offering exceptional value and biblical encouragement to the masses.*

ecpa Member of the
Evangelical Christian
Publishers Association

Printed in the United States of America.
5 4 3 2 1

# Making Memories

by Janet Lee Barton

## Dedication

To my Lord and Savior for showing me the way
and to my family—I thank the Lord for you daily.
I love you all!

# Chapter 1

When Amanda Forrester left the Rosewood Realty office for the day, it was with a huge grin on her face. Not only had she been to closings on the first two houses she'd sold, she'd also received her first listing for the company she worked for. Maybe her move to Oklahoma City hadn't been a mistake after all.

As she got in her car and started for home, she decided to stop at the grocery and buy a steak to celebrate. Maybe she'd buy two and ask Josh Randall, her next-door neighbor, to join her. Actually, she hoped he'd offer to cook them. She hadn't quite gotten the hang of her gas grill yet, and he could grill anything blindfolded.

Amanda rushed into the store and picked out two thick ribeyes. Normally she loved to go up and down the aisles to see everything the grocery offered. It was so much larger than what she was used to back home. But then, everything here in the city was larger than she was used to. She'd been raised on a farm outside of Pierce City, Missouri, and had been a little apprehensive about moving to a city, but she liked to think she was beginning to adjust to it all.

She paid for the steaks and hurried back to her car. As she drove out of the large parking lot and headed home, Amanda realized she should have called Josh to make sure he didn't have plans for the evening. She sure hoped he was free. A celebration meant more if it was shared with someone else. She turned down her street and grinned—Josh was pulling into his drive just ahead of her. She couldn't have timed things better if she'd planned them.

"Hey, lady, need any help?" he asked as he jogged across the small side yard that separated their driveways and their condos.

"Sure." Amanda began to pull bags out of her car. "And, if you'll do the grilling tonight, I'll provide the steaks."

"Steaks?" Josh looked into the bag she handed him.

"Whoa. What are we celebrating?"

"Oh, just my first listing for Rosewood Realty *and* two closings today."

"Wow! That is something to celebrate. I'll be glad to cook for you," he said with a grin.

His lopsided smile never failed to make her feel a little breathless, but as usual, she tried to ignore it. "Sure you don't want to cook inside? It's kind of chilly out."

"Are you kidding? When you have that wonderful stainless steel grill outside?"

"Yeah, and you know the only reason I have that state-of-the-art grill is because some lucky salesman knew I didn't have a clue what I was looking for."

"Well, you made an excellent decision, to my way of thinking," Josh said, taking another bag from her.

"You are going to have to teach me how to use my own grill one of these days, Josh. It thinks you own it."

Josh laughed as he followed her inside to her kitchen and put the two bags he held down on the counter. "I like it better than my own."

"You've used it *more* than you have your own," Amanda teased him.

"That I have. It's a great grill. What time do you want me to start cooking?"

"Let's get them started in about an hour and a half.

I'll put some potatoes in the oven to bake and make a salad."

"Okay. I'll go get changed and check my e-mail. I'll be back in a little while."

" 'Kay. Oh, and would you bring back some sour cream when you come over, if you have any? I seem to have forgotten that."

"See? That's what you get for going grocery shopping without me. I'll bring some." Josh chuckled on his way out the door.

He was right. When they went together, he always prompted her to remember things she might be out of. They'd become good friends when he'd offered to come show her how to light her grill right after she moved in. He'd been in his small backyard next door and had heard her talking to herself—or more accurately, to her grill, trying to convince it to light for her.

She'd offered to share her steak with him that night, and since then they seemed to eat together several nights a week. Josh wasn't shy about asking himself to supper. On the other hand, he was very generous with his help. In the few months she'd lived next door, he'd fixed two leaky faucets—one in the kitchen and one outside. He changed the oil in her car to save her money and he always carried in her groceries if he was around and saw her unloading her car. He'd also told her the best places to shop, the best place to get her car filled up, and he'd even given her the names of his doctor and dentist.

All in all, he'd made the move away from her family a little easier. Much as she hated to admit it even to herself, she did get lonesome at times. She missed her relatives—but not their constant matchmaking.

After each of the cousins she'd been so close to moved away during the past few years—for various reasons of their own—she'd found it impossible to stay in her hometown of Pierce City, Missouri, any longer. With her three cousins gone, her big family suddenly seemed to decide it was their mission to find Amanda a mate. From her parents to her aunts and uncles, they all were determined to find a husband for Amanda.

It didn't matter that she'd told them she wasn't interested. She'd witnessed enough of her cousins' broken romances to know that she'd rather stay single than go through all the heartache they'd endured. She didn't want to hurt her family—she knew their intentions were good—but she just couldn't stay there and go along with their matchmaking plans to set her up with every available man they knew.

So, Amanda opted for moving from Pierce City to Oklahoma City. She felt she really needed to be on her own for a while before she even thought about getting married. Thankfully, she'd been fairly successful at selling real estate at home, in spite of the devastation caused by the tornado that had destroyed most of the historical downtown in 2003. A good part of the town had already been rebuilt and she was happy about that. But when she decided to make the move, she was glad to be able to use her hometown broker's connections to help her find an agency to work for in Oklahoma. After taking the required tests and paying her fees, she'd gone to work for Rosewood Realty as soon as she moved here.

Her parents hadn't been thrilled about the move, but they'd supported her anyway and helped her get settled into her condo in northwest Oklahoma City. But, after they left for home and she was truly on her own, she'd found getting started in a strange city wasn't all that easy. It'd taken a while before she sold her first house and even longer to get a listing of her own. Today truly was a day to rejoice in. She was glad Josh would be there to celebrate with her. Amanda put the foil-wrapped potatoes in the oven and went to change clothes.

She liked her condo and she liked the neighborhood it was in. It was quiet and peaceful. There was a community pool she'd used a couple of times before it got too cold, and there was a walking trail she enjoyed almost daily.

Most of all, she liked her next-door neighbor— probably a little too much for her own good. Josh was the kind of man she could fall in love with if she wasn't careful. He was fun to be with, very nice looking, and, best of all, he was a Christian. She'd been delighted, after meeting him the week after she moved in, to find that he was also in her Sunday school class at church. They seemed to find more and more in common with each passing day. They both liked old movies and the cooking channel on TV. Josh was one of the few men she knew who also liked to shop. Every day she seemed to learn more about him and she liked all of it.

But, she had to remind herself that he was just a very good neighbor—at most a really great friend. He'd shown no sign of wanting their relationship to be any- thing else and Amanda told herself she wanted things to stay just like they were. She certainly didn't want to lose the friendship they shared.

She changed into a soft yellow velour jogging suit and went back to the kitchen to make the salad and dry rub the steaks with a spicy mixture of seasonings. She set the round table in her dining area and turned the gas log on low. Her fireplace was a two-sided one that could be seen from the living and dining rooms at the same time and she really enjoyed it.

The doorbell rang and she hurried to answer it, knowing it would be Josh. She could feel that the temperature outside had dropped as soon as she opened the door to him. "Come on in. It's getting colder. Maybe we'd better cook on my little electric grill tonight."

"Nah, it'll be fine. I'm dressed for it," Josh said. He had on a heavier jacket than she'd seen him in before. Still, it didn't look *that* warm to her. "Are you sure?"

"I'm sure. I've gone to all kinds of tailgating parties this time of year." He handed her a small white tub. "Here's the sour cream you asked for. Now," he said as he squared his shoulders and grinned at her, "lead me to those steaks."

Amanda chuckled and led the way back to the kitchen, shaking her head. Men. They were so funny sometimes.

❧

Josh followed Amanda to the kitchen wondering how long it was going to take her to realize that he wanted to be more than just a good neighbor to her. He'd been attracted to her from the first moment he'd met her. He smiled just remembering the day he'd heard her trying very hard to persuade her new grill to light. Finally, he'd peeked over the fence to find her with an instruction book in one hand and a long-handled lighter in the other. He'd watched for a moment as she flicked the gas switch and put the lighter to it. Then she quickly turned the switch back off. She did the same thing several times before he decided she needed help.

"Hi." He'd called her attention away from her frustration, but he could tell from the way she caught her breath and held her hand over her heart that he'd also frightened her. "I'm sorry. I didn't mean to scare you. I'm Josh Randall, your next-door neighbor. Can I help you there?"

"Oh." She'd let out a huge breath. "Yes, if you don't mind. I can't seem to get the thing started and that salesman promised me it was very easy to light."

Josh was already on his way over through their respective gates. "I'll see what I can do."

She'd given him the lighter and opened the instruction booklet. "Here are the instructions—"

"I think I've got it," he'd said as he bent down and twisted the propane tank on, turned the igniter to the burner, and it lit. The flame was visible.

"Ohh." She began to laugh. "I forgot to turn the tank on, didn't I?"

He really liked that she could laugh at herself. "That's all it was."

"Well, thank you, Josh Randall. I'm Amanda Forrester." She'd smiled, held out her hand, and he'd taken it in his. It was small and soft, and he hadn't wanted to let go of it. But she'd gently pulled it out of his grasp and smiled at him. "Would you like to share my steak with me? It's really more than I can eat."

He wasn't about to turn down a dinner invitation from his lovely new neighbor. "I'd like that a lot. Can I bring anything over? Or cook the steak for you?"

She'd chuckled as she looked at her new grill. "Maybe you'd better."

"I'd be glad to." That evening had been the beginning of a friendship that he secretly hoped would grow into something much closer. He could fall very hard for Amanda Forrester, but she'd shown no sign of being any more attracted to him than she was to any of the other men in their Sunday school class, and he certainly didn't want to harm the friendship they shared now. His life had become much more meaningful with her in it.

"Here," Amanda said, shoving the steaks at him

and bringing him out of his thoughts. "If you are determined to get a chill, go right ahead. I, on the other hand, am going to stay inside and stay warm."

He loved that spunky side of her. She looked so cute standing there with her arms crossed, he wanted to pull her into his arms and kiss her. Instead, he just grinned and saluted before heading outside, determined to grill the best steak she'd ever tasted.

∞

Amanda sighed and shook her head as she watched Josh shut the door against the cold. She put on a pot of coffee. He was liable to want a cup after standing outside for over ten minutes. She tossed the salad and put it back in the fridge, then went to the back door and looked out through the blinds. She couldn't help but smile. He looked so endearing out there leaning against one of the brick columns that held up her patio cover. She watched as he lifted the grill lid and turned the steaks over. Then he seemed to shiver and warm his hands over the heat. She shook her head and grabbed her jacket from the back of one of the bar stools where she'd left it earlier and went to pour him a cup of coffee. The least she could do for a man braving the cold to cook a good meal for her was take his coffee to him.

His eyes lit up at the sight of her, and he eagerly grabbed the mug she handed him and took a sip. "Thank you. This hits the spot."

"Not too cold for you?"

"Nah. Good grilling weather."

She raised an eyebrow at him as he pulled the collar of his jacket up a little higher on his neck, but he only laughed and raised the grill lid again. She sniffed appreciatively. Those steaks did smell wonderful.

"They are almost done. Another five minutes."

"Okay. I'll go get everything on the table." Amanda headed back inside, trying to ignore the thought that she wished they ate together every night.

# Chapter 2

The steak was cooked to perfection. She should probably give him her grill. It just didn't work for her the way it worked for him.

"Mmm, this is wonderful, Josh."

"Thank you, ma'am. I aim to please." He grinned at her before taking another bite.

"Tell me about the Thanksgiving dinner we're helping with at church. What is it we are supposed to do?"

"Just serve, I believe. Our congregation is large enough that we can feed a lot of people in the fellowship hall. The ladies have things so organized that all we have to do is show up and serve those who are less fortunate. The church bus drivers established pick up places years ago and once word gets out about the day and time, they bring full busloads of people right to us each year."

"I just think that is so wonderful." Thanksgiving was the next week and Amanda had been fighting a wave of homesickness for the past few days. She was glad to have something to keep her busy that day. Her family had tried to talk her into coming home for the holiday, but she felt too vulnerable to go. Her mother would be able to tell that she was homesick and she'd have to tell her dad, and he'd insist that Amanda just come on back home. Besides, they'd already started pushing for her to be there for Christmas. She didn't even want to think about that until after Thanksgiving.

"We'll eat there, of course," Josh continued. "It's a good feeling to know you are helping others, but I've always come home knowing I was helped every bit as much as anyone I'd served."

Amanda's respect for Josh raised another notch higher than it had when she found out he was a high school teacher, and she found herself looking forward to serving Thanksgiving dinner right alongside him. Then she wondered if maybe her heart would be safer if she went home for Thanksgiving instead of sharing the day with Josh. She really had to have a talk with herself. For years, she'd been telling her family that she wasn't interested in finding a mate, and now here she was, right next door to a man who seemed the answer to her secret dreams—when she allowed herself to contemplate those things.

"Well, I always make it a habit to count my blessings, but this Thanksgiving I'll have even more to count—a wonderful new home, a great place to work, and a new best friend who knows how to cook the best steak in town."

"Thank you. I have to give some credit to your grill, though," Josh said, smiling at her.

Amanda shook her head and grinned. "You and that grill."

The telephone rang just as they were finishing their dinner and Amanda sighed when she saw the number on her caller ID. It was Granny Forrester. Her parents had called in the big gun. For a moment she was tempted not to answer the phone but then she'd have to explain to Josh. She quickly picked up the receiver. "Hello?"

"Hello, Amanda dear. How are you?" her grandmother asked.

"Hi, Granny! I'm fine. How are you?"

"Well, I'd be doing a lot better if you'd just come on home for Thanksgiving."

"Oh, Granny. I'd sure like to see you all, too, but—"

"Now, Amanda, you know your mama and daddy are going to be really lonesome if you aren't here."

"I've explained it all to them, Granny. They understand that—"

"That's what they say. But I know they are very disappointed that you won't be here."

"Granny," Amanda said as gently as she could, frustrated as she was, "I really need to stay here this year. It's not like I'm never coming home again."

"Then you'll be here for Christmas?"

"I don't know, Granny. I'm just beginning to get settled here and—"

"Now, Amanda Jean, it's one thing for you not to be here for Thanksgiving, but we're all expecting you to be here for Christmas."

Uh-oh. She'd used her middle name. Still, Amanda tried once more. "Granny, I just don't know—"

"Well, you'd better be making up your mind to be here. That's all I have to say. I love you, darlin'. Talk to you later." With that, her grandmother hung up on her.

Amanda didn't know whether to be upset or relieved. She replaced the receiver on its base and let out a huge sigh. Turning back to Josh, she found that he nearly had the kitchen cleaned up. Oh yes. He was going to make some woman a terrific husband.

"You didn't have to do that, Josh," she said.

"Not a problem." He finished wiping off the table. "You bought the steaks."

"And you cooked."

He shrugged. "I felt funny listening in on your conversation. I figured I'd do better to find something to do."

"It was my grandmother. The family is disappointed that I'm not coming home for Thanksgiving and I think they put her up to calling to convince me to come—or at least that's what I thought at first. Now I think maybe they are just starting the campaign to get me to come home for Christmas."

"Oh. It must be nice to have a big family."

Amanda felt bad. When she'd asked Josh if he was going home for Thanksgiving, he'd told her that he'd lost both of his parents in an automobile accident several years before and he was an only child. His aunts and uncles lived on the West Coast and he rarely talked to them. How ironic it was that here he was wishing *for* family and she was trying to avoid hers.

"It is, most of the time. Mine just seems to be a little too. . ."

"Controlling? Meddlesome? Nosy?" Josh chuckled as he teased.

"All of the above. And, sometimes, all at the same time."

"Oh. I see."

Amanda laughed. Somehow she didn't think he did but that was okay. "But, they are wonderful and I love them. I do miss them, too. I just think I need to be on my own a while before I go back home."

Josh nodded as he leaned against her kitchen counter. "It's not easy to be alone for the first time, is it?"

"No, it's not." *But you've made it a lot easier than I expected it to be.* Amanda caught her breath, thinking for a minute that she'd spoken her thought out loud.

"It will get easier, with time," Josh said in answer to her words, not her thinking.

She sighed with relief that her thought was still only that. "I hope so. Want some more coffee? I have some cookies to go with it."

"Sure. I'd love some."

∽

Josh would have liked to hear more about Amanda's family, but she didn't seem to want to talk about them anymore so he didn't press it. From what she'd told him, he knew she came from a large, loving family; and he could tell she missed them. Maybe talking about them made it worse and he certainly didn't want to make things harder on her. The last thing he wanted was for Amanda to get so homesick that she decided to move back to Missouri. So, when she changed the subject, he went right along with her.

"How was your day?"

"The kids are all ready for the Thanksgiving break, and they are always a little high-spirited this time of year." He chuckled. "Actually, that's putting it mildly. But it was a good day."

"Much as I like teens, I don't think I could teach a whole room of them. You must have a special calling to be able to."

He shrugged. "I like it—most of the time. Every once in a while I wonder what I was thinking when I decided I wanted to be a teacher. But I don't believe I'd be as happy doing anything else. I love teaching."

"Well, if my opinion counts for anything, your students are very lucky to have you."

Josh laughed heartily at that. If she only knew how very much her opinion counted. "I wish they all thought the same thing, but I have a couple of students who certainly would not agree with you."

"No."

"Yes." He began to tell her stories that had her

laughing and then shaking her head at some of his students' antics.

When he left an hour later, Josh pulled up his collar and sprinted across the lawn to his own home. It had turned colder while he was at Amanda's. He lit the gas log in his fireplace before hanging his jacket in the coat closet. Dropping down into his favorite chair, he picked up the TV remote control but only stared at the blank TV screen. He would have liked to stay at her place a little longer but he certainly didn't want to wear out his welcome. He loved spending time with Amanda. She had a way of putting sunshine in any day for him.

And she didn't have a clue how he felt; he was sure of that. Or at least, if she did, she didn't want to deal with it. She'd called him a best friend tonight and while he was glad she thought of him in that way, he was afraid that's all he'd ever be to her.

But he wasn't going to just give up without taking it to the One who was in control. He bowed his head and prayed. "Dear Lord, You know how I feel about Amanda. I can't help but believe You brought her here so that we could meet. Maybe I've got it all wrong, and if so, please let me know, Lord. If I'm right, please let her have an idea of what Your plans for us are. And please help me to be patient until that time. In Jesus' name I pray, amen."

He felt better about it all as he reminded himself that the Lord would guide him in this. In the meantime, he had a pile of papers to grade. Josh got up and went to his computer. They certainly weren't going to grade themselves.

# Chapter 3

The next week passed fairly fast for Amanda. She'd been surprised that there were several people from out of town who were relocating after the first of the year and wanted to look at homes that week. Since she was working the desk when they called about a listing, she was busy showing them properties up until Thanksgiving Day and was hopeful of a sale before the end of the week.

She'd also been busy trying *not* to feel guilty about not going home for Thanksgiving, as well as fighting a wave of homesickness just thinking about all the family favorites she'd be missing. Josh had called the night before and made arrangements to take her to church with him and that had helped some—at least until her family called that morning.

She could hear the unhappiness in her parents' voices as they'd wished her a happy Thanksgiving and told her how much they would miss having her with the whole family.

They were all gathering at one of her uncles' homes this year. Thanksgiving was always at a different family member's home while Christmas Eve was always at Granny Forrester's.

In an effort to try to inject a little humor into the conversation, Amanda asked if her aunt Sally was going to make the dressing. It was an inner-family joke ever since the time Aunt Sally had accidentally put too much sage in the dressing. It was almost Christmas green and about as inedible as a tree, too.

She was rewarded by a chuckle from her dad. "No, thankfully. Your mother is making it this year." Amanda heard his leather chair shift as he leaned back, and she pictured him at his desk in the den.

"And it won't be nearly as good with you not here to taste test it for me," Amanda's mother said from the telephone in her kitchen.

"Oh, Mom. You don't need me to taste it for you.

You make the best dressing in the family." And she did. Amanda was certain she wouldn't have dressing anywhere near as good as her mother's.

"Well, I count on you to tell me when I've put enough seasoning in."

"Dad can do the same thing."

"I'll help you, dear." Her dad's reassurance to her mom made Amanda miss them even more.

"Thank you, dear. Amanda, you are going to be with others today, aren't you?"

Her mother seemed to need extra convincing that she wouldn't be alone. "Yes, Mom. Remember, I told you that our church is serving dinner today—"

"Oh yes, I do remember it. And you are going with a neighbor?"

"Yes." She looked at her watch. "In fact, we should be leaving in just a little while."

"Well, you have a great day, dear. We'll be thinking about you."

Amanda was near tearing up, knowing her family would miss her as much as she missed them. But she didn't want them to know how close to crying she was. "You two have a happy Thanksgiving, too. I'd better go finish getting ready. I'll talk to you later, okay?"

"All right, dear. We love you," her mother said.

"Yes we do. And, Amanda?"

"Yes, Dad?"

"You really need to think about coming home for Christmas. I know you are trying to be all independent and grown-up, but—"

The doorbell rang just then, and Amanda literally felt saved by the bell as she honestly told her parents that she had to answer the door.

"I love you both and I'll call later, okay?" She quickly hung up the telephone and breathed a sigh of relief. She just was not ready to even think about Christmas right now. She almost ran to open the door and didn't think she'd ever been quite so happy to see Josh. He looked wonderful, dressed in black pants and wearing a rust-colored sweater over a black shirt.

"Hey, lady, you ready to go?"

She loved the way Josh called her "lady." It always made her feel special. "I am."

"You sure look pretty today," he said, his glance taking in her outfit. "Very. . .Thanksgiving-ish. I don't think that's a real word, but it fits."

Amanda felt herself blush at his compliment. She'd dressed with extra care, choosing a pumpkin-colored dress with brown accessories, telling herself that she wanted to look good for the people they were serving. But deep down she knew she wanted to look good for Josh. "Thank you. You don't look bad, yourself. We almost match, don't we?"

"That we do. Shall we go?"

"Just let me get my purse and coat."

"It's cold out," Josh said, taking her coat from her and helping her on with it. He settled the collar around her neck and his touch sent a sudden charge of electricity down her neck.

Thankfully, he opened the door and she could excuse her shiver as due to the cold air that swept inside. "You are right. It is cold."

"We'll warm up once they put us to work at church," Josh said, helping her into his car. "It'll be nonstop for a couple of hours at least."

That's what she needed, Amanda thought—to stay too busy to think about missing her family and too busy to think about how glad she was to be spending the day with her handsome neighbor.

∽◌∾

This Thanksgiving was turning out to be the best he'd

had in a very long time and Josh was certain it was due to the woman beside him. Her sweet gentleness with the people they were serving settled her even deeper into his heart.

"There you go," she said to one of the ladies in line as she heaped a large spoonful of dressing onto her plate. "Happy Thanksgiving to you."

"And God bless you," the lady replied before moving down the line. As he'd anticipated, they'd been serving nonstop for the past hour and a half, and from the look of the line, the next pair of servers might be there just as long.

"We're here to relieve you," Melinda Benson said, stepping up behind Amanda.

"Oh, is it that time, already?" Amanda asked, looking at her watch.

Andrew, Melinda's husband, held out his hand for Josh's mashed-potato serving spoon. "Has it been like this long?"

"Since the start," Josh answered him with a grin.

"Well, go get something to eat. The ladies outdid themselves this year," Andrew said.

Josh relinquished his spoon and waited for Amanda to do the same before they headed to the kitchen where they could help themselves to the same dinner they'd been serving, without having to get in line. Tables were set up for the volunteers to eat at and after they filled their plates, they joined the rest of the first shift.

The deacon heading up the volunteers said a prayer of thanksgiving, thanking the Lord for all their many blessings and for the volunteers who were willing to give up their family dinners to help those less fortunate. Then it was time to enjoy the meal that had been whetting their appetites while they served.

"Mmm. This is wonderful," Amanda said. "The dressing tastes almost like my mom's and is every bit as good as hers."

"I'm sure she's a wonderful cook, then. I like the sweet potatoes, too. But then I like everything," Josh said.

"It's all just wonderful. I don't know how I'm going to tell my mother that I didn't miss out on any of my favorite dishes," Amanda said. "As unhappy as they were that I didn't make it home for Thanksgiving, I'm not sure she'll be thrilled to hear how good the meal is."

Trisha Lane chuckled from across the table. "I know what you mean. It's kind of like they want you to have a great meal, just not as good as the one you'd have had at home."

Amanda nodded. "Exactly. And truthfully, I'd love to be with them, too. But I haven't been on my own that long and I feel I need to—"

"Get used to that before you got back home," Trisha stated.

"Yes. How did you know?"

"I've gone through the very same thing. And I was so homesick at times, I cried myself to sleep, but I felt I had to stick it out. Now I can go home and come back, and I'm happy in both places. I can't wait to get there and can't wait to come home."

"Oh, that makes me feel so much better, Trisha."

Josh just listened to the conversation between the two women. He was finding out more about Amanda's feelings about being away from family than she'd ever told him.

"I guess I feel even worse because I'm not the only one in the family who isn't there this Thanksgiving," she continued. "Three of my cousins have moved away, also. I'm sure our family feels as if we've all deserted them."

"Four of you left home at the same time?" Josh

asked, his brow furrowing. Why would they all have moved away?

Amanda shook her head. "Not at the same time. Casey and Abigail both moved to California—Casey to Cade's Point and Abigail to San Francisco. Then Lauren moved to St. Louis and I came here."

"Well, I guess you can't blame your family for feeling a little forlorn with all of you gone, huh?" Josh couldn't help but feel a little sorry for her relatives.

Amanda shook her head. "I guess not."

"Josh, somehow I don't think you are making Amanda feel any better," Trisha said.

One look at Amanda's face told him Trisha was right. "Oh, I'm sorry, Amanda. I—"

"It's okay, Josh."

"No it's not. I didn't mean to make you feel bad. I just—I guess I'm coming from a totally different mindset. With no family to go home to, a big family seems a dream to me."

"I understand. And I do have a very big one. I don't mean to sound ungrateful for them. I love my family."

"I know you do." And he did. He could tell by the way she talked about them that she loved them. And he certainly wasn't upset that she'd decided to stay in

Oklahoma. If she'd gone home to be with them, she wouldn't be here with him. "Personally, I'm glad you didn't go home."

He was rewarded with a small smile and a "Thank you."

But Josh had a feeling that he'd put a damper on her joy of the day and for that he was extremely sorry. Somehow, he'd have to find a way to make it up to her.

# *Chapter 4*

By the time they left the church that evening, Amanda understood what Josh had been talking about earlier in the week. She felt she'd benefited more than those who'd come for the meal. Seeing their humble thankfulness had been a vivid reminder of how blessed she was and she was glad she'd been a part of the serving team.

"What are you doing tomorrow?" Josh asked as he pulled out of the parking lot. "Are you one of those early-bird shoppers?"

Amanda shook her head. "Not me. I'll get my shopping done later. I know I miss some great sales, but I just don't like the frenzied crush."

"Neither do I. I do like the lights going up and

seeing all of that, though. How about I take you to the Oklahoma Christmas Tree Lighting tomorrow evening? Then we can grab a bite to eat at one of the restaurants and take in some of the other events downtown."

"I'd like that. I wasn't sure how the city celebrated the Christmas season."

"Well, this will be only our fifth year for downtown OKC, but it gets nicer each year. Last year was the first year for snow tubing. The youth group from church went one night and had a ball. The kids loved it. And we took them to Braum's Ice Rink in Civic Center Park. I had as much fun as they did."

"I've always wanted to ice-skate, but I've never been quite brave enough to try."

"Oh, we'll have to go one night during the season. I'll teach you."

Amanda loved the thought of Josh teaching her to skate, but the thought of her pulling them both down on the ice gave her doubts. "I'm not sure—"

"You'll love it. Just wait and see."

She had no doubt that she would love skating—or trying to skate—beside Josh. In fact, she was so sure she would enjoy it, Amanda wondered if she would be wise to accept his invitation to teach her how to ice-skate. She wasn't sure she should even be going to the Christmas tree lighting. The more time she spent with Josh, the more time she wanted to spend with him—but not necessarily just as the friend he thought she was.

Still, it was the Christmas season and she was looking forward to finding out how the city celebrated. She tried to tell herself that being with Josh had nothing to do with the excitement she felt just thinking about the next evening. But by the time he pulled into his drive and walked her across to her door, she couldn't deny that she was looking forward to going—mostly because she'd be with him.

"The tree lighting is at six," he said as she unlocked her front door. "How about we leave about five so we can find a good place to view it?"

"That will work for me. I have to meet a couple who want to make an offer on a house I showed them yesterday, but that shouldn't take long. I ought to be home on time."

"Good. But if you see you're running late, just give me a call and I'll pick you up at your office."

"All right."

She really wanted to ask him in for some hot chocolate but her telephone started ringing before she could get the words out of her mouth, and Josh just said a quick, "Good night. I'll see you tomorrow," before he sprinted across the lawn.

Amanda shut the door and hurried to answer the phone.

"Amanda, dear!" her mother said with a lilt in her voice. "I thought you were still gone and I was just about to hang up."

"I just walked in the door, Mom. How was your day?"

Her mother's voice changed slightly, taking on a more somber tone. "Well, it would have been much better with you here, but we managed to be thankful for all of our other blessings."

Amanda stifled the chuckle that wanted to escape. Her mother could be very dramatic on occasion. "I'm glad, Mom. And your dressing turned out great, I bet, didn't it?"

"It was pretty good. At least everyone said it was even better than last year's."

"I knew it would be."

"Did you have dressing, dear?"

"I did. It was different from yours, but it was pretty good." Then she quickly added, "Of course we were starving when we got to eat, so everything tasted real good. But oh, Mom, it was such a blessing to be there today! Since I wasn't with you all, I'm glad I was able to help at church."

"You could have been with us, dear."

Amanda sighed. "I know, Mom. I—"

"Your uncle Jim has a new young man working for him," her mother interrupted. "We think he is just your type and that the two of you would make a wonderful couple."

Of course they did. They thought any available man they met would be perfect for her. "Mom—"

"Really, dear, he's very nice looking and so sweet."

"I'm sure he is, Mom." Amanda could have bit her tongue as soon as the words were out of her mouth. And at her mother's next words, she knew she should have.

"Maybe you can meet him at Christmas."

"I'm still not sure about coming for Christmas."

"Now, Amanda, surely you'll be here for Christmas. We miss you so."

"I . . ." She couldn't deal with this tonight. So Amanda simply opted to put off telling her mother that she had no intention of coming home to meet this new man. "Miss you all, too."

That seemed to satisfy her mother for the moment.

"I am glad you enjoyed helping at church, too. It there a nice group of young people there?"

"Oh, yes, there is a really great young adult group."

"Good. I'm glad. What are you doing tomorrow? I'm going shopping with your aunt Lily. She wants to leave at five in the morning."

"Oh, Mom, I don't know how you get up that early to do that. I'm not going shopping. I have to meet with a client. But, I am going to a tree lighting tomorrow evening."

The conversation turned to trees and how her mother was decorating this year and Amanda was very relieved that her mother didn't get back to whether or not she was coming home for Christmas. Missing them so, she'd been thinking maybe she would go home—until her mother brought up the new man they wanted her to meet. And there was a whole month until Christmas. No telling how many men they'd have lined up by then. Amanda had to find a good reason for not going home again. And she had to find it fast.

∽∾

Josh had been to the city's tree lightings many times in the past, but he'd never had as good a time as he was having tonight. It was all due to Amanda's company.

She was in high spirits when he'd knocked on her door, having made her third sale that day, and her mood had gotten better as the night went on.

She seemed to love the Christmas lights as much as he did as she watched the Oklahoma Christmas Tree Lighting. The sudden burst of twinkling lights when the switch was turned on had the crowd cheering in delight.

"Oh, Josh, isn't it beautiful?" She craned her neck to look up. "It's so big!"

"It's supposed to be the state's tallest cut tree."

"I can believe that. And it's just gorgeous."

And so was Amanda, her blue eyes shining with joy at the profusion of lights.

"Ready to see more of what downtown OKC has to offer?"

"Oh yes!"

Before the evening was over they'd taken a cruise on Bricktown's Water Taxi to see the lights there, then they'd headed over to Braum's Ice Rink in Civic Center Park and watched the skaters. He got Amanda to promise she'd try to skate another night when it wasn't so busy and was just glad she'd agreed to another night out with him. The hot dogs smelled so good they'd decided to have one for supper and go to one of the downtown restaurants another night. Then they took in the Oklahoma Gas and Electric Garden Lights before heading home.

Josh hated to see the evening come to an end, so when he'd walked Amanda to the door and she asked him if he wanted to come in for a cup of hot chocolate, he didn't hesitate to say yes.

He lit the log in her fireplace while she heated the milk and mixed the cocoa and sugar. Then he took a seat at her snack bar and watched as she mixed all the ingredients together and simmered them all until he could inhale their delicious smell. She'd just poured the aromatic liquid into two cups when the telephone rang. He sipped from the cup Amanda handed him and tried not to listen in on the one-sided conversation. But it was impossible not to.

❧

Amanda recognized the telephone number on her caller ID and picked up the receiver quickly. "Hi, Dad!"

"Hi, baby. Your mom said you had a good Thanksgiving but I wanted to check on you myself."

"I had a great day," Amanda said, pretty sure that wasn't the answer her dad was looking for, so she added, "I missed you all, of course."

"We missed you, too. You aren't going to put us through that again at Christmas are you?"

Amanda sighed and shook her head. She should have ignored the call. "Dad, I'm just not sure—"

"Amanda, it will break your mother's heart—not to mention your granny's. Now you just plan on coming home, you hear?"

"Daddy, I'll think about it, okay?"

"Well, you think about it all you want. But we're setting a place for you for Christmas." Then before Amanda even had a chance to reply, he added, "And we expect you to be here. Night, baby. Love you."

"Da—" The click and buzz on the line told her that her dad had said all he'd planned to say. Forgetting for a moment that she wasn't alone, she moaned and put her receiver down a little too hard.

"Whoa. You okay, Amanda?" Josh asked, reminding her that she had company.

More than a little embarrassed at her reaction to the phone call, she forced herself to smile at him. "I'm all right. Just a little. . ."

"Frustrated?" He grinned and raised an eyebrow at her, as if he could read her mind.

"You could say that. I know you wish you had a big family, Josh. And I do truly love mine, and I would love to spend Christmas with them—but I just don't think I can handle any more of their unending matchmaking!"

"Matchmaking?"

"Yes. That's the main reason I left home. They've been trying to marry me off since I graduated. And I do want to get married—one day. But I think I need to be on my own for a while between living with my parents and getting married."

"That makes sense."

"Well, they don't see the need in it. And since my cousin Lauren left home," Amanda continued, "if it wasn't my parents trying to set me up, it was my aunts and uncles. And even Granny got in the picture, introducing me to the man who does her yard work for her. And it's not like I haven't asked them not to—over and over again." She let out a big sigh.

"Oh. I had no idea, Amanda."

"I know. It's just that none of the men they seem to think would be perfect for me have interested me at all. We have nothing in common. So, my family tells me that I'm too picky or too hard to please—even just too stubborn to see that someone they pick could be right for me. I guess maybe I am, but I'd at least like to feel a little spark of attraction for someone." She shook her head. "And besides, it doesn't do much for my ego, with my family thinking that they have to find me a mate. Don't they trust me to find my own, when the time is right?"

"I, ah—"

"I don't think there is anything wrong with refusing to 'date, just for the sake of dating,' do you?"

# Chapter 5

No, of course not! You don't see me dating just for the sake of it, do you?" He didn't add that the only person he wanted to date was her—and dating just to date certainly wasn't something that Josh wanted Amanda to be doing. He wanted to be the one to take her out when she decided she was ready to start seeing someone. And if they did start to date—when they did—he didn't want her to be dating him just to be going out with someone. He wanted it to be because she cared about him.

She'd told him once right after they met that she wasn't interested in blind dates or any other kind of date, and he'd thought maybe she'd suffered from a breakup. Instead, her family had evidently set her up with so many wrong men that she was a little sick of the whole dating scene entirely. He was glad he'd gone slow, fearing that he would scare her off if he let her know how much he cared about her. And yet—perfect timing was one thing, but what if his was off and because of his dawdling, she went home and met someone she could really be interested in?

"That's what I keep telling them," Amanda said, continuing their conversation. "But if I'm stubborn, then I got it from my family because they just don't give up. They probably already have two or three lined up for me to meet if I go home for Christmas. And they've started the campaign to get me there."

He had no doubt that she was right. She hadn't gone home for Thanksgiving and if they'd missed her half as much as he would if she went home, he was certain that her family was going to try to get her to come home for Christmas—to set her up once more. The thought that she would be seeing other men if she went home, and perhaps meet one who did have something in common with her, had Josh's mind whirling with ways to keep that from happening.

Amanda stirred her cooling hot chocolate and sighed. "I dread going so much, but I know they won't let up until I agree."

Josh hesitated for a minute or two before deciding to pitch the idea that came to mind. After all, he was desperate and the stakes were high. If she didn't agree to his idea, he could well lose her. "Why don't I go home with you?"

"They'd think I'd brought you home to meet them, because, well, because, they'd think we're dating here. I can't lie to them, Josh."

"No, and I wouldn't want you to. Why don't you just tell them the truth? Tell them I'm the guy next door and have no place to go for Christmas."

"You don't know what you'd be letting yourself in for, Josh. Before you could even say hello to them, my family will jump on the very fact that I brought you home and have us paired up as a couple."

*Like having them think Amanda and I are serious about each other would bother me.* "Don't worry about that, Amanda. I can handle it if you can."

"Josh, you don't know my family. They'll be planning a wedding before we—" The phone rang again, cutting her off. She looked at the caller ID and moaned. "They've called in the big gun *again*. It's Granny."

She gave a big sigh before answering on the third ring. "Hello, Granny. You're calling awfully late—nothing is wrong is there?"

There was a long pause as Amanda listened to her grandmother. Josh had to stifle a guffaw when she closed her eyes and shook her head. Evidently her grandmother stopped to catch her breath as Amanda said, "Now, Granny, you know I haven't promised to come home—"

*Cut off again,* Josh thought as Amanda's side of the conversation halted. It appeared she was losing ground to the older woman when after several moments of watching Amanda rub her temple, she tried to get another word in, "Oh, Granny—"

Interrupted again, it was a few more minutes before Amanda said, "Really? Do you think they will?"

Then, finally, a chuckle from Amanda. "Oh, all right, Granny. I'll be there to hang my ornament. But I'm bringing a friend with me—my next-door neighbor has no place to go for Christmas."

Another pause and then Amanda grinned. "No, it's not a girl. Josh Randall is my neighbor and I'm bringing him home with me."

Something must have come up at her granny's because the next words out of Amanda's mouth were, "I love you, too. Night."

"No questions about me?" Josh said as she hung up the receiver.

Amanda laughed. "Oh, there will be plenty of questions about you. But right now I'm sure she's calling my parents and then everyone else in the family to let them know I have a man in my life." She quirked a delicate eyebrow at him. "Are you sure you're ready for this?"

Not only was he ready, he couldn't wait to meet Amanda's family. "I think so. I know I will be by the time we leave. What made you change your mind and tell her you'd come?"

"Well, your offer to go with me helped. But if you could have heard her. . ." Amanda shook her head. "I didn't have a chance. She pulled out all the stops: She and the whole family miss me terribly; she may not be here next year. . . . I thought that was hitting below the belt, but that's Granny for you."

"Oh, I can see how that would get your attention."

"Well, as if that wasn't enough—"

"There's more?" Josh asked, chuckling.

"There is always more. But she's trying to talk all three of my cousins into coming home, too, and it will be so great to see them, if they do. And, hopefully there will be safety in numbers for us all."

Maybe she really didn't need him to go if the cousins were going to be there, but Josh wasn't about to mention that thought. He was quite happy that she'd told her grandmother that he was coming with her. Surely she wouldn't change her mind.

❧

By the next evening, Amanda had a few misgivings about taking Josh home with her for Christmas. She'd had calls from her parents and her grandmother again. They were thrilled that she'd decided to come home but, most of all, they were delighted that she was bringing a man with her.

"What is he like, dear?" her mother asked.

"He's a very good neighbor, Mom. But we're just friends. He has no family to go home to."

"Oh, the poor dear. Well, we will try to make up for that. What does he look like?"

"Oh, he's tall and broad shouldered. He has dark hair and blue eyes. He's nice looking."

"Hmm. And what does he do for a living?"

"He's a schoolteacher, Mom."

"A teacher?"

"Yes. He teaches high school."

"How nice! And you met how?"

"Mom, we live next door to each other and I was having trouble with my gas grill. He came over and helped me light it."

"I see. He came to your rescue. I can't wait to meet him."

"Mother, we are only friends. That's all."

"I understand, dear."

She might understand the words, but Amanda knew her mother well and her mother's next words didn't surprise her at all.

"You know your dad and I started out being best friends, too."

"I'd forgotten, I guess," Amanda said. How could she have forgotten that? It was going to be harder than ever to convince her mother that she and Josh were only friends, now. Still, she had to try. "But not everyone is like you and Dad, Mom. You two were meant to be together."

"Yes we were. And you never know where friendship will take you, dear. We're all looking forward to meeting your young man."

"Mother!"

"I'm sorry, dear. I meant to say your *friend*. I'll give the spare room a good cleaning. Are there any dishes he particularly likes, dear?"

"Mom, Josh will like anything you make. He's not picky and he's very easygoing." As Amanda spoke the words, she realized how true they were.

Her call-waiting beeped and she looked at the caller ID. It was her grandmother. "Mom, that's Granny on the other line. I'll call you back, okay?"

"No need to call me back tonight. I'll talk to you later in the week, dear. Love you."

"Love you."

Amanda clicked over to her grandmother's call. "Hi, Granny!"

"Hello, Amanda dear. I won't keep you but a minute. I just wanted to know if you thought I should make your friend an ornament to put on the tree."

"Granny, that's up to you. But keep in mind that we are just friends and you'd need to let him bring it home with him."

"Oh, of course I would, dear. I just thought it would make him feel more a part of things."

"Whatever you want to do is fine, Granny." They all had their own special collection of wooden ornaments to hang on her grandmother's tree and each new member of the family was provided with one. It would be nice for Josh to have something to hang on the tree, but she knew her grandmother was trying to find out if they were more than just good friends.

"His name is Josh, isn't that what you said?"

"Yes, it is."

"Well, I'm looking forward to meeting him. I just wish all of you girls would settle down and have some great-grandchildren for me before I leave this land."

"Oh, Granny. Now, don't you be counting on me for that. Josh and I are just good neighbors."

"And he had no place else to go?"

"No, ma'am. His parents have passed away and he was an only child."

"Oh, dear, we'll have to make this Christmas special for him."

"He wouldn't want anyone to go to any extra trouble, Granny. I'm sure he's just glad not to have to spend Christmas alone."

They talked for a few more minutes, but Amanda ended the call as soon as she could. The more she talked, the more her grandmother was going to think there was more to her and Josh's relationship than there really was.

Dear that Josh was, he truly didn't know what he was letting himself in for. Her family could be loud and boisterous and loving, and she wasn't sure Josh was ready for them. She should probably let him out of his offer. By the time they arrived at her parents', her family would probably already have the wedding planned—and that would present more problems down the road.

Maybe she could cancel at the last minute. If she did it now, she'd have no peace. But she did want to be part of the family Christmas, to hang her special ornament at Granny's, and to see her cousins.

And with Josh along it would be such a blessing to go home and not dread being "fixed up." Nonetheless, she was sure that even though she would say Josh was just a friend, her family would assume that he was more, because of the very fact that she was bringing him home with her. To them that would mean she must care about him, and they certainly wouldn't hinder what they thought might become a serious relationship.

By the time her family actually figured out that there was no romance, it would be time to come home. Or, better yet, maybe they would continue to think that she and Josh might be serious about each other—at least enough so that they would quit matchmaking for a while.

Oh, what a blessing that would be!

She found herself looking forward to introducing her family to Josh. She knew they would like him. She just hoped they wouldn't be too much for him. She knew her cousins would take a liking to him and, for a moment, she couldn't help wishing she'd been able to introduce him as the man she was dating instead of just her next-door neighbor.

Josh found he was looking forward to Christmas more than he had in years. He'd spent more of them alone than he cared to think about and he wondered what being with a huge family like Amanda's would be like. Aside from the matchmaking—which he didn't like the idea of any more than Amanda did—he was sure they were a warm and loving family. It would be enlightening to see them together.

He wondered if he should buy gifts for everyone or just for her parents and started to pick up the telephone to call Amanda and ask but then decided to run next door and talk to her. She opened the door almost immediately, and he could tell she was on her way out or just getting home.

"Hi! Did I catch you at a bad time? Are you coming in or going somewhere?"

"I was just about to go out to the store. I wanted to take some cookies in to work tomorrow and I'm out of nuts."

"Well, come on. I'll run you to the store—if you'll let me taste test those cookies."

"That's a deal."

It wasn't until they were on their way that Amanda asked, "What were you coming over for? Did you need to borrow something?"

"No. I wanted some gift ideas for your family." Just as he figured, she shook her head.

"Josh, you don't need to take presents."

"I know I don't have to, but I really would like to. I haven't spent a Christmas with a large group in so long. I'm really looking forward to it."

Amanda chuckled. "I'm glad. But I'm not sure you'll feel the same way after you've heard my dad's hunting stories for the fiftieth time."

"He likes to hunt? What kind of hunting does he like to do?"

"Just about any kind. He likes to fish best but not in the wintertime."

*Hunting and fishing. Her dad shouldn't be too hard to buy for.* "Does your mother have any hobbies?"

"She loves to cook, just like we do. And she likes to read."

*A cookbook for Mom.* "What about Granny?"

"Granny likes everything. She loves to cook. She loved to sew, but her eyes aren't quite as good as they used to be, so she does all kinds of other crafts. Crocheting is a favorite. And she loves to fish, too."

*Well, Granny shouldn't be too hard to buy for, either.*

"But really, Josh. They don't expect you to get them anything. They are just thrilled you are bringing me home for Christmas."

Josh smiled as he turned into the parking lot of the grocery store. They couldn't be any more pleased than he was. Christmas with Amanda and her family—the prospect had him almost as excited as a kid.

# Chapter 6

W ant to help me put up my tree tonight?"
Josh asked as she got out of her car the
next evening. "I'll order pizza."

"That sounds like fun. I'd love to. I'll bring cookies."

"I was hoping you would."

The walnut chocolate chip cookies she'd made the
night before were delicious. It was a good thing she'd
made a double batch. "What time do you want me to
come over?"

"As soon as you get changed and grab the cookies."
He grinned. "The tree came with pre-strung lights and
I have it up. I just need some help spreading out the
branches so it looks real and then we can put on all the
ornaments."

"I'll be right over." She hurried into her house and quickly changed into jeans and a sweatshirt decorated with Christmas trees of varying sizes. She'd been planning on putting her own tree up that evening, but it would be much more fun to help Josh. Maybe he'd return the favor and help her decorate hers another time.

She filled a ziplock plastic bag with cookies, slipped on her jacket, and hurried over to Josh's condo. She was always a little surprised when she went inside his home. It had a definite masculine feel, yet felt very warm and homey at the same time. The rich brown-leather sectional faced the corner fireplace. His tree stood beside the fireplace and it was huge. It had to be at least eight feet tall and once all the branches were arranged it would be very full.

The lights were lit and Josh had already added the topper. He'd started pulling out the branches to give it more shape and make it look fuller. "Just step right up and start wherever you want. I have some gloves, if you'd like to put them on. The needles are a little sharp. They make these trees seem real these days, don't they?"

Amanda pulled on the gloves he handed her. "They certainly have improved them. I love real trees, and my parents insist on one, but they are expensive and so I decided to buy an artificial one. Want to help me decorate mine tomorrow night? I'll make a pot of soup and maybe more cookies."

"Sure. I'd be glad to help you."

They sung carols with the Christmas CD Josh had put on as they shaped the tree and put on the ornaments he'd brought out earlier in plastic boxes. He had quite a collection started.

Just as he placed the last brightly painted ornament on the tree the doorbell rang and Josh went to answer it. The pizza deliveryman's timing was perfect. Josh pulled some bills out of his pocket and thanked the man before closing the door and turning to Amanda.

"Let's eat in here so we can enjoy the tree." Josh set the wonderful-smelling box on the oversized ottoman in front of his sofa. "I'll get paper plates and some soft drinks and be right back."

He was back in a flash and set the ottoman with a flourish before flipping open the pizza box. "Mmm, smells delicious, doesn't it?"

"It certainly does. I never realize I'm so hungry for pizza until I get the first whiff of a freshly baked one."

They each helped themselves to a slice and settled against the sofa to look at the tree while they ate.

"I know a lot of people wouldn't put up a tree if

they weren't going to be here for Christmas Day," Amanda said, "but I just love looking at the lights at night."

"So do I."

"I'm not sure mine will compete with your tree, though. It's lovely, Josh."

"That's because you helped with the ornaments. I usually manage to have them all on one side or the other, and it nearly always looks a little lopsided."

Amanda chuckled just picturing it. "Well, it's not lopsided tonight. I bought one of those stands that rotate the tree all around. I hope it works right."

"We'll get it to work," Josh said.

Amanda found herself looking forward to the next night and putting up her own tree. Having Josh there to help would make it an even more special event.

"Does your family have any special traditions at Christmas?"

"Well, my cousins and I have always spent Christmas morning at Granny's, where we have hot chocolate and rolls with her and then hang our special ornaments on her tree. Then that night the whole family gathers there again to open presents and celebrate Christmas with her. The next day will be at my parents' house, where we'll open more presents and have Christmas dinner."

"No." Josh shook his head. "I'm sure I'll love it all. I'm just glad to have somewhere to go."

Amanda was still having second thoughts about this—thinking her family might overwhelm him or that he might be wishing he hadn't volunteered to go—but thinking about him spending the day alone made her glad that he was going.

"I love turning out the lights and just leaving the tree lights on," Josh said as they finished the pizza. He flipped off the lamp on the end table and the lights on the tree seemed to glow brighter. "Isn't that beautiful?"

"Yes, it is," Amanda said. With the Christmas music in the background and the twinkling lights, sitting side by side on the sofa took on a different feel. There was something warm and cozy and. . .kind of romantic about the moment. But they were just friends. Amanda jumped up and began gathering their plates and glasses. "I guess I'd better be going. Surprisingly, I'm showing houses again tomorrow morning."

Her appointment with her clients wasn't until eleven the next morning, but suddenly she felt a need to go home. She and Josh were just good friends and she didn't want to ruin their great relationship by weaving dreams that were unlikely to come true.

Josh walked Amanda to her house, wondering why she'd suddenly decided to hurry home. It was only nine o'clock. Maybe she was just tired of his company—but it didn't seem that way as she told him not to forget about the next night.

"Oh, I'm not likely to forget. Soup and cookies, right?"

"Right."

"You didn't stay long enough to have any of the ones you brought over tonight."

"Those are yours; you enjoy them."

"Thank you—for the cookies and for helping me tonight."

"It was fun. I enjoyed it."

"So did I." It was getting cooler out and he didn't want her catching cold. Since she didn't ask him in, he turned to go. "See you tomorrow."

"At six, okay?"

"Six it is." He turned and waved before jogging over to his place. It had been a wonderful evening to his way of thinking. Trimming a tree with Amanda made all the difference in the fun of it all. But he couldn't help wondering if he'd done the right thing by pushing her to take him home for Christmas.

Maybe she was having second thoughts. He certainly hoped not. As he entered the living room and looked at the tree glowing brightly in the otherwise dark room, it dawned on him that he might have scared her off by turning off the lamp. It had felt just right to him to be sitting beside her, admiring their work. But he had to admit he would have liked to have put his arm around her as they sat there—would have liked to thank her for helping him. . .with a kiss.

He shook his head. There was no denying that he cared about Amanda a great deal. In fact, he was sure he was falling in love with her, but he didn't want to ruin the relationship they enjoyed now. He wasn't sure what to do. Should he let her know that his feelings for her were growing or just pretend that they were best friends? Maybe during this trip the Lord would make things clearer to him and he would know what to do.

∽

Amanda found herself looking forward to decorating her tree with Josh so much that she decided it would be best to invite most of their Sunday school class over, too—with others around it wouldn't seem nearly as romantic as the night before. When she called Josh to let him know, he seemed pleased and she didn't know whether to be glad or disappointed that he didn't appear to mind that they wouldn't be spending the evening alone.

She baked all afternoon—three different kinds of cookies, plus corn-bread sticks to go with the soup she had simmering when the first guests arrived. Trisha Lane came with Mark Edwards. They'd only been dating for a few weeks. Josh came over next, and then Andrew and Melinda Benson showed up. John and Carey Reynolds were also there, as were most of the rest of their class.

But even in a room full of people, Amanda was aware of Josh's every move. And he never seemed very far away from her. He took charge of putting the tree into the revolving stand and he was there to help her put the topper on the tree. She liked the way he just pitched in and helped her serve dinner, standing by her side and handing out the bowls after she ladled soup into them. And it felt natural and right to have him by her side. For a minute, she let herself think of how it would feel if they were a couple like Trisha and Mark, but she quickly shook that thought out of her mind. The fact that he was going home with her for Christmas—to keep her family from setting her up with any of the men they'd chosen for her—only meant he was a very good friend coming to her rescue and she needed to keep that in mind.

But that was hard to do, especially when Trisha was helping her make hot chocolate for everyone and bluntly asked, "Are you and Josh seeing each other?"

"We see each other every day just about, Trisha. We live next door to each other."

Trisha threw her a look that said Amanda knew that wasn't what she meant. "You know what I mean. Are you dating?"

Amanda shook her head and tried not to give away how much she wished she could say yes to that question. "No. We aren't dating. We're just really good friends." And that's probably all they'd ever be, much as she was realizing she'd like there to be more—but she wasn't going to tell Trisha that. And even though her mother had said she and Amanda's dad had started out as best friends, Amanda just wasn't sure how you could get around the friendship phase into the romantic phase—and she didn't know if Josh would even want to try to get there.

"Well, I'm glad you asked him to go home with you for Christmas. He sounds really excited about it. I can't imagine what it would be like to have no family to share the season with."

Amanda was a little surprised that Josh had mentioned it to the others and relieved that he hadn't told them exactly why he had offered to go. She didn't want everyone to know that her family seemed to think she needed help in the romance department. "No, neither can I," she agreed with Trisha. "Not with the huge family I come from. Grab that plate of cookies, will you?" Amanda picked up the tray of hot-chocolate mugs, and they rejoined the party.

Josh was at her side to take the heavy tray from her. "Mmm, this smells delicious," he said before placing it on the coffee table so her guests could help themselves. "What is a tree-trimming party without hot chocolate?"

Her tree did look pretty. It wasn't decorated with the homemade wooden ornaments like her grandmother's was, nor the sequined balls that her mother liked, but it suited her just fine. She liked the painted glass ornaments that Josh used so much that she had gone out and bought some for her own tree. She loved the way the lights picked up the different-colored Santa Clauses and snowmen. And the revolving tree stand worked beautifully.

"I'm going to have to get us one of those stands next year," Melinda said. "I love the way the lights seem to twinkle as it goes around."

"I do, too," Amanda said.

"It makes it easier to decorate, too," Mark said. "You only have to stand in one spot and let the tree turn to you."

All in all, the evening was a huge success, and in some ways it was even more romantic than the night before—with Josh staying behind to help her straighten up after everyone else left. He brought empty cups to her and helped her load the dishwasher.

"It was a nice night. Everyone seemed to enjoy themselves, don't you think?"

"I'm sure they did. I know I enjoyed it," Josh assured her as he placed the last cup in the rack.

"So did I," Amanda said, thinking that this is what it would be like if they were married, talking over their evening with friends, and—Amanda clamped down on that unexpected thought. Where had it come from?

## Chapter 7

Amanda didn't want Josh to go home. She wanted to sit beside him and look at her tree lights in a dimly lit room. She wanted him to pull her into his arms and kiss her. But Josh seemed to have other ideas. He put on his jacket as soon as they went back to the living room, and she tried to hide her disappointment.

He stood looking at the tree as he buttoned up. "Your tree looks really great, Amanda."

"Thanks to all of you. I couldn't have done it by myself. Thank you for getting it into the stand. I don't think I'd have been able to do it without help."

"You're welcome. I was glad to help. We have the same taste in ornaments; do you know that?"

Amanda chuckled. "I do. In fact, I liked yours so well I decided to start my own collection of the same kind. I hope you don't mind."

"Not at all." Josh shook his head as he walked to the door. "How about helping me shop for Christmas? We could go to Quail Springs Mall and maybe take in a movie one night this week."

Her heart expanded with happiness at his invitation. "Sure. I have some shopping to do, too. And at least it won't be quite the crush of the day-after-Thanksgiving shopping."

"Okay, how about Monday evening?"

"Sounds good to me."

He opened the door and turned back to her. "Want to ride to church with me tomorrow?"

"Sure."

"I'll warm the car up before I come and get you."

"You don't have to—"

"It's cold outside." Josh cut off her protest. "You don't need to see me out. I'll see you in the morning." He gave a wave and closed the door behind him.

Amanda locked the door and leaned against it. It wasn't the perfect end to the evening but at least they'd be spending time together the next few days. And it was really better that he hadn't stayed. It was getting harder to pretend all she felt for him was friendship. Here she was, picturing them as a married couple!

Her family was going to fall in love with him. Of that she had no doubt. He'd be helping her mother and grandmother with anything they requested of him and he'd be talking to her dad and uncles about the football games, hunting, fishing—anything they wanted to talk about. And that presented another problem. They'd like him so much they'd be really disappointed when they realized that she and Josh really were only good friends.

She pushed away from the door and told herself she should probably just let Josh out of his offer to go to Granny's with her for Christmas. But she didn't want to. She wanted him to go—and not only to keep the matchmakers at bay. She loved being with him and she wanted him to have a good Christmas, too. He must be looking forward to it or he wouldn't have mentioned it to their Sunday school class. Much as she wished his reason was because he wanted to be with her as much as she wanted to be with him, Amanda was pretty sure that he simply wanted to experience what Christmas was like with her big family. Well, it appeared he was going to find out.

∽

As Josh sat looking at his Christmas tree, he wished

Amanda were there with him. He hadn't wanted to leave her place tonight. He was looking forward to spending Christmas with her and her family more each day. But he was having a hard time pretending that the reason he wanted to go was to help her out. It was more that he felt he was protecting his own interests. But how was he ever going to be able to let her know that? He had a feeling he wouldn't be accompanying her home for Christmas if he did. And if he did, would he ruin what they shared now? He sighed deeply. He didn't know what to do except leave it all in the Lord's hands. Surely, He'd let him know if the time was ever right to let Amanda know he was falling in love with her.

He chuckled to himself, thinking about her asking if he minded that she'd decorated her tree similar to his. How could he mind? It was just one more thing they had in common. He wondered if Amanda realized how many of the same things they liked. Each day he seemed to find more that they had in common. They would make a great couple; he was sure of it. Maybe one day Amanda would see it, too. In the meantime, Josh was going to enjoy each and every minute with her.

On Monday they went to Quail Springs Mall and began their shopping. For Amanda's mom, he found a cookbook they both wanted by one of their favorite food-network cooks. Amanda bought her mother computer software so that she could adjust her recipes to any amount depending on how many she was cooking for. She also mentioned that she would like to have it herself so her mom had better like it, and Josh made a mental note to go back and get one for her.

They browsed for presents for the aunts and uncles and cousins, but as they were both starving, they decided to do the shopping for them on the coming weekend.

They went to a nearby Italian restaurant for supper and Josh was glad when they were shown to a table for two in a secluded corner. After they'd given their orders to the waiter, he quizzed Amanda about what Christmas was like with all of her family.

"It's fun most of the time. But it's loud. Everyone seems to talk at once."

Amanda chuckled, making him think that she really didn't mind it. Her next words told him he was right.

"We pride ourselves on being able to keep up with several conversations at one time. Are you sure you're ready for all this? How many conversations can you keep up with at a time?"

Josh leaned back in the booth and grinned at her. "You forget—I teach high school."

"Oh, that's right. Well, you'll fit right in, then. My dad and uncles tease us all about it, but they love it. They pretend not to hear, but they listen in often. We know, because they'll say, 'Huh? What did you say?' if they miss anything."

Josh had to chuckle. "They sound fun."

"They are for the most part. And I do love them all very much, in spite of the meddling, the matchmaking, and the never-ending advice."

"I'm sure they love you very much and only want what they think is best for you," he said. From what he'd heard about her family, Josh found himself eager to meet them. He could only hope that he would measure up in their eyes.

"I know they do. I just wish they would trust that I can figure out what's best for me on my own—with the help of the Lord."

Josh also hoped that she would come to realize— with the help of the Lord—that *he* was best for her.

Once their appetites were sated, they continued their shopping. For Amanda's dad, they went to a sporting goods store and Josh found a book on how to make the flies he loved to fish with. Josh added some special supplies to make them, hoping that they weren't any her dad already had.

After that, they went to a huge craft-supply shop in the area and found some specialty thread that Amanda assured him Granny would love. They stopped for hot chocolate on the way home and Josh couldn't remember when he'd enjoyed shopping for Christmas so much. Of course he'd never had much shopping to do—and then it was mostly for a few friends and coworkers. This was different and much more special. He wasn't sure what to get Amanda, but he wanted it to be something she would keep always. He'd kept her so busy helping him decide what to get her dad and grandmother, he hadn't been able to get a clue on what to get her other than the recipe software. He'd get that, too, but it wasn't quite special enough. He resolved to watch her closely on their next shopping expedition to try to get an idea or two.

Amanda got ready for bed that night thinking that she had never had such a good time Christmas shopping. It was so different going with a man. Josh wanted so much to get something special for each person and he hadn't settled for anything less. She knew her parents and grandmother were going to love the presents he had picked out for them. She was more convinced than ever that her mother and Granny were going to fall in love with Josh right off the bat. How could they not? She was having a hard time resisting that very thing.

Amanda was afraid she was dangerously close to losing her heart to him. Why had she let herself think that bringing Josh home for Christmas would make things easier for her? Oh, it would put a stop to the matchmaking for the time being, but only until her family realized that she and Josh were truly only friends. No, in the long run, it was going to make things much harder because she didn't know how she was ever going to be able to hide her growing feelings for him. And what if she couldn't? What would that do to their friendship?

"Dear Lord, please help me *not* to fall completely in love with Josh. I don't want to ruin the relationship we have now and I'm not sure it could survive if he knew I was thinking of him romantically. Please help me to stop thinking of him that way and especially help me not to let him or my family know that I have been. In Jesus' name, amen."

She should never have accepted his offer, but now he seemed so happy and excited about spending Christmas with her family that there was no way she could change her mind—especially now that he'd bought them gifts. She'd just have to make the best of it and pray that she and Josh came back to Oklahoma City with their friendship intact.

# Chapter 8

The next weekend the Bensons threw a Christmas party for their Sunday school class and Josh seemed to just naturally assume Amanda would ride with him. She knew she probably should have taken her own automobile, but she couldn't bring herself to turn down a warmed-up car and his company. Besides, it was fun showing up at the party together as if they were a couple, and most of the class had begun to treat them as if they were one.

" 'Bout time you two showed up," Melissa said. "We've been waiting on you to get started."

"Started on what?" Amanda asked, looking around the living room. She couldn't see that anything needed to be done. The tree was decorated beautifully, as were the mantel and the rest of the house as they passed through the dining room to the family room.

"We're going to have a gingerbread-house contest. Come on out to the kitchen, everyone, and I'll hand out the makings," Melissa said.

"What fun! I haven't made a gingerbread house in years," Amanda said.

"I've never made one in my life," Josh said, "but it sounds like fun."

"We don't actually have to make the gingerbread, do we?" Trisha asked.

"No. I bought these kits from a local bakery," Melissa answered as she and Andrew began handing them out, one box to each couple, or in the case of singles, pairing them with another as a team to work together. "The directions are on the box and I have extra icing, gumdrops, and other candies, so you have no excuse not to make a dazzling house."

Amanda was more than pleased when she and Josh were paired together and sent off to one of the small folding tables that had been set up for each team.

"Do we get to eat these when we are finished?" Mark asked.

"No," Andrew said. "We'll be giving them to the children of some of the members who are receiving Christmas baskets from the church. A lot of folks are having a hard time making ends meet this year."

"Oh, well that is a good cause. Guess I'll resist the temptation to nibble as I work."

"Don't worry, Mark. The pizza man will be showing up at any time, and I made desserts this afternoon," Melissa assured him.

"I'm glad she told us she was feeding us," Josh whispered to Amanda. "I probably would have done a little taste testing myself."

Amanda only chuckled as they got to work on their house. Josh turned out to be very adept at cementing the walls together with icing. The roof was another matter, though. It took several minutes to get it to line up just right. Then the fun part began as they decorated the small cottage.

"I just love gingerbread houses. I saw a beautiful glass gingerbread-house decoration the other day, but it was a bit more than I wanted to spend for a tree ornament. It was lovely, though. It was so detailed and colorful. Maybe next year I'll feel like I can get one like it since I won't have so much to buy."

"It sounds great. Do you remember where you saw it?" Josh asked as he lined the walk with red and green gumdrops.

"No." Amanda shook her head. "I think it was at one of the stores in the mall, but I just can't remember. You would like it, too, though. It would go great with your collection."

Josh nodded and looked thoughtful for a moment. "Maybe on our next shopping expedition we'll find out where you saw it."

"I do need to pick out a few more things, but you don't need to feel you have to go with me." Then, thinking that sounded rude—as if she didn't want him with her—she added, "Unless you have shopping to do for others. But I don't want you thinking that you need to do any more shopping for my family."

"I have a few more things to get. How about we go on Monday evening to finish up? We're leaving next weekend, right?"

Amanda nodded, trying to ignore the little shiver of anticipation that ran down her spine. She put icing on two small candy canes and put them on either side of the front door. "I thought we could leave on Friday after-noon, if that's all right with you. That way I'd be there in time to go to Granny's the next morning like always."

"That's fine. We can leave earlier if you decide you'd like to. School is out until after the New Year, so I'm free as a bird until then. I can't begin to tell you how much I'm looking forward to meeting your family."

And that was the reason she could not—and would not—back out of accepting his offer to go with her. His excitement about sharing Christmas with her family was almost contagious, or at least that's what she kept telling herself that her growing excitement about the trip was all about.

The doorbell rang and Melissa and Andrew hurried to answer it.

"Pizza man!" Melissa called back to them. "It's time to take a break and gather round the kitchen island."

"She's not going to have to call me twice," Mark said.

"Nor me," Josh added.

"We ought to have a gingerbread-house judge to see who's made the prettiest one. I think Mark and I would win," Trisha said.

Amanda craned her neck around to look at their project and shook her head. "No way. Mine and Josh's would win."

They were in the middle of teasing rivalry when Andrew and Melissa came back with the pizzas.

"Look at that," Andrew said. "Leave them without food too long and they revert to their childhood. We'd better feed them quick or they're liable to get quite cranky." Once he said the blessing for the food, it didn't take long to empty the last box of pizza.

Eating did seem to settle them all down before they went back to their house making. By the end of the evening, Amanda figured it was a good thing their projects weren't judged—they were all adorable and she prayed that the children who received them would be delighted.

Amanda and Josh stayed after everyone else left so that they could help Melissa and Andrew straighten up the family room and kitchen, and pack up the houses they'd all made. As the women packed the gingerbread houses in deep pastry boxes to be taken to church and given out, Josh and Andrew took them out to the Bensons' vehicle. They came back in from one trip to the garage laughing and disappeared into the front of the house before coming back for another box.

"What are you two up to?" Melissa asked her husband.

"You'll see later." Andrew winked at her and gave her a kiss on the cheek before they took another box back out to the garage.

"Men." Melissa shook her head and grinned. "No telling what they are plotting."

"You're right about that." Amanda chuckled and

nodded. She'd seen her dad and uncles pull one prank after another often enough to recognize the signs. "We'd better be on our guard."

Melissa insisted that they have a cup of hot chocolate before heading out into the cold night air and Amanda thoroughly enjoyed the next half hour of small talk. She was feeling more and more at home in Oklahoma City and knew that a lot of her ease was due to the three people at the table. She sent up a silent prayer thanking the Lord for sending them into her life.

"I guess we'd better be on our way," Josh said. "We wouldn't want to be late for Sunday school."

"No, that wouldn't be good," Andrew said. "Especially for me as I'm teaching the class this quarter."

Melissa retrieved their coats from the closet in the entryway and Josh helped Amanda with hers before putting on his own.

"Thank you so much for your hospitality," Amanda said to the Bensons as they all stood in the entryway.

"Thank you for coming." Melissa gave her a hug.

Andrew cleared his throat and pointed up to the small chandelier hanging above the women.

There, hanging right above their heads, was a large clump of mistletoe tied to one of the crystals with a red ribbon. Andrew pulled his wife into his arms and planted a quick kiss on her lips as Amanda watched, slightly bemused. Then, before she realized she was still standing in the same spot, Josh had turned her face toward his and touched his lips to hers in a kiss so light and sweet Amanda almost thought she'd imagined it.

"Merry Christmas," he whispered.

"Merry Christmas," Amanda found her voice and whispered back.

"So that's what you two were up to," Melissa said with a chuckle. "I should have guessed."

Amanda felt her face flushing with embarrassment— and what she hoped no one knew was pure happiness.

# Chapter 9

Amanda was so quiet on the way home that Josh was afraid he might have overstepped the boundaries of their friendship by kissing her. But that clump of mistletoe was too good of an opportunity to pass up. He hadn't been able to resist the chance to kiss her.

Now he could only pray that he hadn't ruined things. He hadn't been able to tell how she felt about his kiss. Oh, color had flushed her face, but he didn't know if it was because she was surprised by his kiss—or angry. And yet, for a second he thought he'd felt her lips cling to his. But maybe that was because it's what he wanted to believe. At any rate, he was doing way too much thinking when he should be trying to break the silence in the car.

"Amanda?"

"Yes?"

"I think our gingerbread house was the best one."

She gave a soft chuckle and the tightness in his chest eased a bit. "I think so, too. I'd forgotten how much fun it was to decorate one."

"It was a first for me, but I really enjoyed it." *Just not nearly as much as I enjoyed kissing you.* He pulled into his drive and shut off the engine. "Want to ride to Sunday school with me tomorrow?"

Amanda hesitated for only a minute before answering. "Sure. It does seem a little silly for us to take two cars when we're going to the same place, doesn't it?"

"It does." Josh met her coming around the back of his car and they walked briskly over to her front door. It felt as if the temperature was falling by the minute. "I'll have the car warmed up, too."

Amanda grinned at him in the glow of her porch light. "That's one of the perks of riding with you—a toasty car."

"I aim to please," he said as she unlocked her door and turned back to him. She looked so pretty looking up at him; Josh wanted to kiss her again. But there was no mistletoe hanging over her head and he wasn't sure what her reaction would be. So, he just gave her a wave as he turned to go. "See you in the morning."

"See you then."

❧

Amanda shut the door, her heartbeat still fluttering, as it had been ever since Josh's kiss. She told herself not to read too much into it. Kissing under the mistletoe was only a Christmas tradition. It meant nothing.

Well, that wasn't entirely true. It meant a lot to her. It meant she could no longer deny her feelings for Josh—certainly not to herself and most probably not to her family. And in about a week she was going to have to pretend that they were *only* friends when she knew she wanted more. And how did *that* happen, anyway? She hadn't wanted to fall in love with anyone—didn't want her family finding her a mate. She'd wanted to be on her own a while before she even thought about marriage. She'd lived in her parents' house all her life and felt like she should at least be able to support herself and know what it was to make a living before she settled into a relationship. Or so she thought.

Now all she could think of was the man next door and what it would be like to be able to introduce him to her family as the man she was going to marry. Yet, until the kiss tonight, Josh hadn't shown that he felt anything more toward her than friendship. And she really didn't think that tonight was an exception. He most probably was just carrying out a simple tradition. She wanted to think the kiss meant something to him, but how could she find out without putting their friendship on the line? They lived next door to each other, went to the same church, and enjoyed each other's company now. If he felt uncomfortable about her growing feelings for him, how long would that last?

And if he felt uncomfortable, how much more so would she feel? She might have to change churches just when she was feeling at home—might have to move to keep from seeing him each day.

Amanda moaned and sent up a silent prayer. *Dear Lord, what have I done by letting myself fall in love with my best friend here? I don't want to lose the friendship we have. But if it's possible that he could care for me, too, please help me to know. And if it's not, please help me to be able to hide how I feel from him and from my family. In Jesus' name, I pray, amen.*

☙

Their Monday night shopping trip had to be canceled because Amanda had a surprisingly busy day with new clients who were moving to the area right after the New Year and wanted to find a house. She was hoping to end the week with a sale, and Josh was hopeful that she would, but he missed her company.

With their trip to her hometown nearly upon them, Amanda insisted that he go on with his shopping trip. It was nowhere near as much fun as shopping with her had been. Since she wasn't with him to show him the decoration she'd liked so much, Josh visited every store he thought might have it but left without that special present for her.

He spent the next few days trying to find the perfect gift for Amanda and had about given up when he decided to visit a Christmas store in a mall on the other side of the city. When he finally spotted the colorful glass gingerbread-house ornament that looked like the one Amanda had described to him, he couldn't resist. If for no other reason, he wanted to get it for her to remind her of the night they'd made the houses and kissed under the mistletoe. It even looked a little like the gingerbread house they'd made together. He browsed the aisles to see what else he could find and then he spotted the perfect ornament for the two of them—if their relationship ever got to the point he'd prayed for. To the point where he could tell Amanda how much he loved her.

The delicate glass ornaments were small but detailed clumps of mistletoe that looked real. They would be sure to make them both remember the first time he kissed her. Josh didn't know when he would give Amanda one—a lot depended on this Christmas with her. But he bought two. He knew he wanted one for his tree and hoped with all his heart that one day they would be able to put both ornaments on the same tree. In case that didn't happen, he wanted to make sure that each time Amanda put the ornament on her tree through the years, she would think of him.

They'd planned on getting together that afternoon and evening to finish Amanda's shopping, and then they planned to wrap the presents for her family at her place. Josh carefully wrapped the gifts he'd bought Amanda that morning and slipped them into a bag. He felt as if he'd finally found presents that would let Amanda know how special she was to him. He could only pray that he was special to her in the same way.

# Chapter 10

Amanda and Josh ended their final Christmas shopping trip with a meal at one of their favorite Mexican restaurants before going back to Amanda's to wrap presents. When they got home, Josh ran into his place to pick up the presents he'd already bought and brought them back over to Amanda's so they could get all their wrapping done together.

When Josh rang the doorbell, Amanda opened it to find his hands full of bags of the gifts they'd picked for her family and her heart melted. He was so sweet to want to choose gifts that were just right for them. "Come on into the kitchen. I have paper, tape, ribbon, and bows all laid out on the table."

She had the makings for hot chocolate ready and a

plate of the cookies she knew Josh loved nearby. They'd barely gotten started with their wrapping before the telephone rang. She could tell from her caller ID just who it was. "Hi, Granny!"

"Have you been watching the weather, Amanda dear?"

"Well, no, should I be?" Granny loved to watch the weather channel on TV just as much as Amanda and Josh liked to watch the cooking channel.

"They are calling for a major snowstorm to move in. You might want to leave a little earlier than you'd planned. You don't want to get caught in it."

"No, we wouldn't want to do that," she assured her grandmother. "We'll watch the weather forecast and make a decision, okay?"

"All right, dear. And you be sure to tell your young man to drive carefully."

"He's not—" Amanda clamped her mouth shut on the denial. Josh might not know it, but she wished with all her heart that he *was* her young man. "He'll be careful, Granny. I'll see you Christmas Eve morning, okay?"

When she hung up, she went to get the TV remote so they could get the weather forecast. "Granny says bad weather may be moving in and she thinks we should leave earlier."

"Oh?" Josh stopped his wrapping and watched the news with her. There was, indeed, a chance for bad weather moving in before Saturday. "Maybe your grandmother is right. It might be best if we leave tomorrow. What do you think?"

She was all packed for their trip, except for the presents that would be put in the back of his car. "Well, I can be ready. But will it be an imposition for you if we leave earlier? It will mean one more day with my family and they—"

"Amanda, I am looking forward to Christmas with your family. It can't get started early enough for me."

She'd tried to warn him on more than one occasion that her family could be overwhelming. But she had a feeling that if anyone could handle her family, it would be Josh Randall. "Well, then I'll leave the decision on when to leave up to you."

"Okay. We'll finish our gift wrapping and keep listening to the weather, but if things don't change, I think we need to leave no later than tomorrow morning."

"Okay." Amanda had been looking forward to the three-and-a-half- to four-hour trip home in Josh's car. She certainly wasn't going to complain about leaving early. She'd just have to be on her toes and not give away how much she cared about him.

They'd decided to leave Friday morning, and as Josh put his and Amanda's luggage in the trunk of his car and the colorfully wrapped presents in the backseat, he couldn't believe how excited he was about this trip. He'd made up his mind that at some point during this visit with her family, he was going to have to let Amanda know how he felt about her. He prayed she felt the same way about him, but if not, he'd have to depend on the Lord to help him through the hurt. He just couldn't keep spending time with her without falling more and more deeply in love with her, and it was time to find out if she could ever feel the same way about him.

Amanda looked so pretty today. She was dressed in jeans and a bright red sweater; her blond hair was pulled back from her face and her blue eyes were bright and shining. She could protest all she wanted, but he had a feeling she couldn't wait to see her family again.

"Buckle up," he said as she got in the car.

"Yes, sir!" She saluted as she pulled her seat belt around and secured it. "It is looking like snow, isn't it?"

Josh backed out of the drive and headed toward the turnpike. He looked out the window and nodded. "I think it may be a fast-moving storm. I hope we're leaving in time to dodge it."

He turned the radio to a station that was playing Christmas music and before long they were both singing along with the familiar songs. They were on the other side of Tulsa when it started to snow. Beautiful as the big flakes flying at them were, Josh hoped it got no worse. He could see where they were going now, but the snow was sticking and he feared the roads could become dangerous if they didn't drive out of it soon.

"Oh, isn't it pretty, Josh?" Amanda asked. "I hope we have enough at home to make a snowman. I love playing in the snow."

"It's beautiful," he agreed. He looked forward to helping her make that snowman. It'd been a very long time since he'd felt so happy this time of year, and he knew his happiness was because of the woman sitting beside him. He'd been looking forward to sharing Christmas with her and her family for weeks now, and he prayed that they liked him and that before this visit was over, their matchmaking days for Amanda would end.

But until then, he needed to know how she wanted him to act when he met her family for the first time.

"Amanda, when we meet your parents—how are you going to introduce me?" The snow was falling fast and steady now. He couldn't take his eyes off the road but he listened closely for her answer.

"Why, as my next-door neighbor who had nowhere to go, like we planned. Josh, it's getting worse out there. Can you see the road?"

"For now I can. Will that keep them from trying to set you up with someone while we are there?"

"Well, I figure that no matter what I tell them, they are going to assume we are—" Wind hit the car and whipped it to the side. "Josh—"

"I'm going to have to pull to the side of the road, Amanda. It's getting too bad to see and if I don't do it now, I won't know where the edge of the highway is." Josh couldn't see behind them, either, but he didn't want to tell her that. He eased over to what he hoped was the shoulder of the road and safely out of harm's way.

But Josh had no more than applied the flashers on the car when the sound of screeching brakes came from behind them and made his heartbeat thud in his chest. He quickly grabbed Amanda and pulled her into his arms. Bracing for the crash he was sure was coming, he sent up a silent prayer. *Dear Lord, please let us get out of this alive.*

The expected crash never came. Only a whooshing kind of sound was heard as a vehicle flew past them and then there was a sudden silence.

"Josh?" Amanda eased out of his arms.

"We're all right, but I don't know—" They looked around to find the automobile that had come off the road behind them, stopped down the embankment just shy of a tree.

Josh and Amanda left his car almost at the same time. They rushed over to the car and Josh thought he heard a sob as the driver opened the door. "We're all right. We're all right."

Josh peeked inside and saw a badly shaken woman trying to calm two young children. But they were, indeed, all right. *Thank You, Lord.*

"Do you need any help getting out of here?" Josh asked the man.

"No, I don't think so. I just hit a really slick spot back there. I think the car is all right. I'll turn it around and pull in behind you."

"I have some cookies in our car, if you think the children would like them," Amanda said to the woman. Tears were streaming down the woman's face, in what must have been relief, as she nodded.

Amanda took off toward his car, and Josh followed. By the time the man had the car back on the shoulder, Amanda had a bag of cookies ready.

"I'll take them over," Josh said. "You just stay here and get warm."

"What's this?" Josh asked as he entered the car and shut his door against the cold. Tears were flowing down Amanda's cheeks. "Honey, it's all right. We're okay. That family is all right, too."

Amanda only nodded and sniffed. Josh pulled her back into his arms and she began to sob. "Amanda, we're all right."

"But—but we could have been killed and—I'm so sorry I've pulled you into trying to deceive my family, Josh. I'll understand if you want to turn around and go back to Oklahoma City."

Josh was still shaking on the inside from their close call. Had that car taken a slightly different path, they both could have been killed and he would have died without ever letting Amanda know how he felt. He sent a silent prayer upward, thanking the Lord again for watching over them and for giving him another chance to tell Amanda that he loved her.

"Amanda, you didn't pull me in. I offered to come with you. The last thing I want to do is turn around and go back home. Besides, you can't take the blame for the weather. I was the one who should have realized we needed to leave earlier. If anything had happened to you, I would never have been able to forgive myself."

Still sniffling, Amanda looked up at him with those big, tear-filled eyes. "I promise you, I'll make sure my family knows that you aren't in love with me as soon as we get there so you won't feel any pressure to act as if you are."

Josh pulled her into his arms. He had to tell her now. "Oh, Amanda, I can assure you that letting your family think I'm in love with you won't be an act."

He heard her quick intake of breath but he didn't give her a chance to say anything. His lips claimed hers in a kiss he hoped left no doubt in her mind just how he felt. His heart sang with joy when she kissed him back. Knowing Amanda as he'd come to over the past few months, Josh was sure she wouldn't have responded the way she did if she didn't feel the same way.

When she ended the kiss and pulled back, Josh reached into the backseat and pulled a small package out of one of the sacks. "Here; open this."

Amanda ripped open the paper and opened the box the mistletoe ornament came in. She pulled it out and held it to her heart. "Mistletoe."

"I wanted you to always remember our first kiss when you hang that ornament. And I've been hoping that it would be hung on *our* tree one day." He hurried to say the words that he'd wanted to say for weeks.

"I love you, Amanda—with all my heart. And if you are willing, we can tell your parents a simple truth—that we are engaged. Will you marry me?"

Amanda answered him with another kiss that told him all he needed to know, before she even said anything. When it ended, she whispered, "Oh, Josh, I love you, too. I've loved you for weeks—and yes, oh yes! I will marry you."

❧

Amanda had never been happier in her life than when she and Josh pulled into her parents' drive and hurried up the porch steps. The front door was opened before they got there and her parents welcomed them with open arms.

"I'm so glad you got here safely. We heard there've been several accidents due to the storm," her mother said, giving her a hug and trying to pull Josh into it, as well.

"We had a close call, but it turned out to be a blessing," Amanda said. "Mom, Dad, I'd like to introduce you to my fiancé, Josh Randall."

As her dad shook Josh's hand and her mother gave him a bear hug, Amanda thanked the Lord above for seeing them home safely and for giving her the best

Christmas ever. Tomorrow she and Josh would join her family at Granny's to carry on her family's tradition, but they'd already begun to make special Christmas memories of their very own.

## JANET LEE BARTON

Janet has lived all over the southern U.S., but she and her husband plan to now stay put in Oklahoma. With three daughters and six grandchildren between them, they feel blessed to have at least one daughter and her family living in the same town. Janet loves being able to share her faith through her writing. Happily married to her very own hero, she is ever thankful that the Lord brought Dan into her life, and she wants to write stories that show that the love between a man and a woman is at its best when the relationship is built with God at the center. She's very happy that the kind of romances the Lord has called her to write can be read by and shared with women of all ages, from teenagers to grandmothers alike.

# Dreaming of a White Christmas

by Kathleen Miller

# Dedication

To Brittany Bodden, Kristy Bodden, Sally Miller,
Meagan Holman, Lauren Adams, Megan Adams,
Alison Goss, and Sarah Goss, my precious nieces. . .
may the Lord always lead you and guide you.

*And the angel said unto them, Fear not: for, behold,
I bring you good tidings of great joy, which shall be to
all people. For unto you is born this day in the city of
David a Saviour, which is Christ the Lord. And this
shall be a sign unto you; Ye shall find the babe wrapped
in swaddling clothes, lying in a manger. And suddenly
there was with the angel a multitude of the heavenly host
praising God, and saying, Glory to God in the highest
and on earth peace, good will toward men.*
LUKE 2:10–14

# Chapter 1

*Cade's Point, California—Thanksgiving Eve*

I t's the day before Thanksgiving and I'm sitting in a store window up to my eyeballs in work."

Ducking beneath the swag of brilliant green tinsel, Casey Forrester surveyed her progress as she suppressed a yawn. It must be near to midnight. She'd know the exact time if she hadn't lost her watch somewhere in the simulated red snow.

Casey leaned against the paper-covered glass of Callahan & Callahan's easternmost window. *Honey, you're a long way from the Ozarks, but this is a whole*

*lot better than a double helping of Granny's turkey and
Aunt Lou's pumpkin pie.*

All right. So it wasn't really better, but if she repeated
the thought enough it might push away some of her
homesickness. After all, she was doing exactly what
she'd always wanted to do: design store windows.

And how bad could it be to have all your dreams
come true in a place where palm trees and beaches
were the standard scenery? After all, Cade's Point had
the benefit of being situated comfortably between Los
Angeles and Malibu on the Pacific Coast Highway.
While their neighbors to the north and south paid city
prices for their oversized homes, the post–World War
II beach shacks and bungalows bordering Riverside
and Cade's Beach Boulevard could be had for a steal.

Someday she would make one of those lovely cot-
tages hers. Until then, she'd settle for two rooms and a
bath in a converted attic across from the beach. If she
stood on the toilet and craned her neck, she could see
Cade's Beach and the glorious Pacific beyond.

"Sun, sand, and a view of the beach from my
bathroom window. What could be more perfect?" She
stumbled over a cable, then righted herself by reaching
for the first of three blue tin trees. "All right, I admit it,

Lord. I don't want to be here tonight. I'm tired." Casey punctuated the statement with a yawn.

Obviously the Lord wanted her here or Mrs. Montero, the store's manager and Elias Callahan's daughter, would never have entrusted Casey with the job of creating the Christmas displays for Callahan & Callahan Fine Clothiers, the most fashionable store on the entire West Coast. Considering this time last year she was planning what to wear to the Christmas formal at Ole Miss, Casey considered herself extremely blessed. Mrs. Montero told her she'd beat out a long line of much more experienced competitors to win the position.

Casey's first assignment: create a drop-dead amazing set of store windows to celebrate Callahan & Callahan's newly remodeled Cade's Point store. The offices where the big brass worked were just two floors up, so Casey had spent the past few months designing windows that would be seen by most of America come Thanksgiving Day under the watchful eyes of everyone from the janitor to the CEO himself, Elias Callahan. At least they *tried* to watch. Mrs. Montero had upped the pressure by electing not to preview Casey's designs and decreeing that anyone caught looking over Casey's shoulder would be summarily dismissed.

Given all the hype, gratefulness at being given her big chance had soon turned to sheer terror at the prospect of messing up. When the three windows of Callahan & Callahan opened on Thanksgiving morning, the whole world would be looking at Casey's work for the first time.

Well, anyone who watched local TV or cable news, anyway.

Fear overtook her, and Casey had to sit. She sank down beside a pile of gifts wrapped in rainbow colors and topped by bows of silver and gold, and rested her head on her knees.

What if the world wasn't ready for her designs? What if she had created a huge flop?

*What will I wear?*

Mrs. Montero told her preview photos of the windows were considered a hot commodity on the Internet. Yesterday, Mr. Riley, a security guard, caught a guy from the *National Questioner* posing as a deliveryman so he could peek at the design.

Brenda from accounting and Liz, the new hire in cosmetics, told her at lunch they'd been approached by e-mail from several journalists offering payment for pictures of the famous Callahan & Callahan windows.

Neither accepted, not that they had any more access to the designs and the actual windows than anyone off the street.

Casey felt her pocket where the keys rested against a partially wrapped peppermint and a note reminding her to grab milk on the way home. As of this afternoon, she held the only key to the three locked windows. Even Mrs. Montero couldn't get in, although in theory she could order Casey to hand over a key anytime she felt the need to peek.

Slowly she rose, then reached down to fluff up the faux snow where her rear had made an impression. One final check of the display Casey called Neon Noel and she tiptoed to the exit hidden behind the brilliant orange bag of toys. The door clicked behind her and she fitted the key into the lock, then rested her forehead on the steel door.

"Lord, what have I done?"

"You've created a right interesting set of windows, I'm sure."

Casey jumped, her breath caught just shy of her throat. Resplendent in his Christmas-green coveralls stood Mr. Riley, a man whose age defied calculation. Rumor was, he'd been hired by the original Callahans, although Mr. Riley refused to confirm or deny this.

"I'm sorry, little lady. I ought not to have spoken without first letting you know I was here." He cocked his head to the side, then pointed to a spot just north of her eyebrows. "Did you mean to have that red fuzz in your hair?"

Swiping at her forehead, she watched a sizable chunk of cherry-colored faux snow land between her sock feet. Casey quickly picked it up and stuffed it into her pocket alongside the mint and note.

"Thanks," she said, as she pushed on the door one more time to be certain it had closed tight. One more window to check and she could call it a night. Or a morning, if it was as late as it seemed.

"If you'll excuse me."

She ducked past Mr. Riley to head to the south end of the building. This side faced the ocean, thus lending itself nicely to a beach theme she'd come to call Sandy Claus.

"You done for the night, Miss Forrester?" he called as she rounded the corner at foundations.

"Not yet," she said, "but you don't have to stay on my account."

It was a well-known fact that Mr. Riley's job was a

token one. The real security for Callahan & Callahan's flagship store was an alarm system handled by a firm out of Los Angeles whose prototype was in use at the governor's mansion in Sacramento.

Casey didn't know he'd caught up with her until he banged his flashlight against the escalator. She jumped.

"You're a skittish thing, aren't you?"

She gulped to slow her racing heart. "Well, sir, I guess I'm just not used to watching a big-time security man like yourself on the job. I sure do appreciate the work you do here, Mr. Riley."

The old man hitched up his coveralls with one hand and gripped his flashlight with the other. "You ain't from around here, are you?"

Well who was? With few exceptions, the folks she'd met since she arrived in town last July were all from somewhere else. The California native seemed as rare as the California condor.

"No, sir," Casey said. "Pierce City, Missouri, by way of Ole Miss."

He gave her an appraising look. "Thought as much."

*Okay.* "Yes, well, if you'll excuse me." She unlocked the door to the beach scene and stepped inside.

"You going to be in here long?" he called.

"Fifteen minutes at the most." She stuck her head out to see him standing where she'd left him. "Were you in a hurry?"

"I don't suppose," he said. "I'll go make my rounds one more time before I leave. Ought to take about fifteen minutes, twenty at the most."

She stepped into the window and reached for an errant elf whose swim trunks had been put on backward. "That should give me plenty of time." A moment later, Casey left the display and locked the door, satisfied that all was well at the North Pole Pier.

One more window, her favorite, awaited her final inspection. She called it Dreaming of a White Christmas, and it was a near-perfect reproduction of Granny Forrester's front parlor back in Pierce City. Complete with a towering, bedecked spruce and gifts wrapped and tagged with the names of her cousins, it boasted a well-worn King James Bible open to the story of the Nativity and a cane rocker just like Granny's. Wooden ornaments sat waiting in a basket on the hearth, a reminder of the Forrester family tradition.

Casey stepped inside and hit the switch, bathing the window-turned-room in a homey combination of warm lamplight and cozy orange firelight from the faux fireplace in the corner. She walked toward the fireplace, marveling that the flames were no more real than the cherry-colored snow in the Neon Noel window.

It seemed as though, if she were only a few feet closer, she could warm her hands by the fire and fill her empty stomach with the freshly melted ingredients for s'mores that waited on the hearth. And the stockings? Exact replicas of the ones she and her cousins hung every year on Christmas Eve.

Closing her eyes, she wondered what Granny Forrester was doing right this minute. Probably sleeping, she decided, for the matriarch of the Forrester family rose before dawn and, in her own words, went to bed with the sun.

Definitely not California hours. Even now Casey could hear the sounds of traffic dashing past on the boulevard.

She shrugged the tiredness from her shoulders, then reached for the crocheted granny-square afghan currently draped on the arm of the plaid sofa. Cuddling the soft material against her cheek, she turned to peruse the details of the room.

Doilies on sofa arms. Check.

Braided rug on floor. Check.

Framed photographs of family. On this she had been forced to compromise. While they weren't actual family members, they would fool just about anyone except her family.

Casey lowered herself into the rocker and arranged the afghan over her legs. Two days until her big debut. She reached for the Bible, a happy find in the back of a dusty shop in the valley, and sighed. Words from the second chapter of Luke rose unbidden in her mind: *"And the angel said unto them, Fear not: for, behold, I bring you good tidings of great joy, which shall be to all people. For unto you is born this day in the city of David a Saviour, which is Christ the Lord."*

She settled deeper into the cushions of the cane rocker and pulled the afghan to her chin, closing the Bible. The firelight beckoned, so she turned her attention there as she suppressed a yawn.

*"And this shall be a sign unto you; ye shall find the babe wrapped in swaddling clothes, lying in a manger. And suddenly there was with the angel a multitude of the heavenly host praising God, and saying, Glory to God in the highest and on earth peace, good will toward. . ."*

A moment later, Casey jerked as something hit the floor with a thud. The Bible. She reached over to set the heavy volume back in its place on the chair-side table, then rose and stretched before heading toward the door.

Stepping out of the window, she walked into total darkness. "What. . . ?"

She reached behind her to open the door, then flipped the switch inside. Light streamed through the opening and lit the space around her.

"Mr. Riley?" When he failed to answer, she called again. "Must not be able to hear me."

Casey took a few steps out of the rectangle of light, then froze. She'd never get anywhere like this.

Ducking back into the window, she grabbed the battery-operated floor lamp and headed for her office in the back of the store. Once there, she snagged her purse and empty lunch bag and made her way to the employee exit. It was locked tight.

"Mr. Riley?"

Still no answer.

Gripping the floor lamp, Casey retraced her route, then turned toward the doors on the east side. They, too, were locked, as were the ones on the south and north sides. Until she found Mr. Riley, she was good and truly locked in, the only alternative being to trip the alarm by opening an emergency door.

In her exhaustion, Casey briefly considered doing just that. Then she took that scenario one step further. Not only would she rouse the security guard and the Cade's Point Police Department, but Mrs. Montero and Mr. Callahan would also be summoned.

Then there was the matter of the press. If anyone saw the windows before the big opening, decades of tradition would be ruined.

Better to ferret out Mr. Riley. Perhaps the elderly fellow had fallen asleep somewhere in the store. Lamp in hand, she set off in search of the security guard who held the key to her exit—literally. Unfortunately, after a half hour of searching and much banging on doors, walls, and other structures, she failed to raise the security guard.

Panic edged into the corners of her mind and threatened to creep further. Casey shook her head and reached into her purse for her cell phone. If she couldn't get out, she could at least call out.

Casey opened the flip phone and punched the green button. Nothing happened.

She tried again. And again. Dead. What a time to realize she hadn't charged her phone.

"Great." Casey closed the phone and dropped it

into her purse. "Now what?"

Using a store line sounded like a great plan, until she realized she had no idea who to call. Back in Pierce City there were any number of folks who would get out of bed to come and rescue her from a locked department store or see her through whatever emergency had befallen her.

But here in the city she knew no one that well. She did have a lunch table companionship established with Brenda from accounting, and Liz from cosmetics had offered a free makeover anytime she desired. Still, a live body across the lunch table and a pal who could hide your dark circles did not equate to a good friend you could call at midnight.

Or whatever time it was.

*If I get out of here with a job, I am going to make sure Brenda and Liz know I'm that kind of friend. If...*

Casey leaned against the locked door and closed her eyes. Now what?

Granny Forrester's parlor beckoned, and she headed back toward the Dreaming of a White Christmas window to settle into the cane rocker. Best-case scenario: Mr. Riley would return to let her out or someone arriving early to work would take pity on her.

Worst case? "Well, I just won't entertain those negative thoughts. The Lord will get me out of this mess. He always does."

She'd nearly fallen asleep when she thought better of it. Staying awake was her only hope for keeping this minor emergency from turning into a major fiasco.

Casey rose and rubbed her eyes. She'd make a pot of coffee up in the break room, then get something to read from the books-and-gifts department. Before she knew it, dawn would break.

Or, better yet, Mr. Riley would come out of hiding and release her.

The coffee made, she carried her mug and the most gripping mystery novel she could find into her office. Settling into her soft leather chair, Casey placed the book in front of her on the desk, then took a sip of strong black coffee.

"This should keep me up."

Half an hour later, she lifted her head off the desk to realize she'd soaked the edges of the novel with the remains of the overturned coffee mug. Casey straightened the mess as best she could and fought to knock the cobwebs from her brain. What to do? She certainly couldn't be caught sleeping at her desk. That would be more embarrassing than sleeping in the window and much more of a public spectacle.

Sleeping in the window. Of course.

She opened her desk drawer and picked up her notepad, then scribbled two notes, one each to her two companions. After placing the notes on their desks, she headed for the Cade's Point Boulevard window where Granny Forrester's parlor waited.

Back in Pierce City, she and her cousins had spent many nights sleeping by the fire. They'd called it camping out. Tonight Casey would be camping out alone, at least until someone came to rescue her.

# Chapter 2

Ben Callahan was a mess and he knew it. That last call, a four-car accident out in Hidden View, had done him in. Between the bumpy ride up the canyon's fire road and the combative patient they'd transported to Valley General, he'd ended up feeling like he ought to be the ambulance's next occupant instead of the EMT.

If he weren't so tired, he'd probably have the strength to count the number of runs the ambulance crew had gone on tonight. It numbered in double digits; this he knew for sure. The last time he'd spent a night like this, he'd been on the other side of the world in a combat zone.

But then, some nights it seemed as though he'd never left the patch-'em-up-and-ship-'em-out mentality of the military. There certainly seemed to be parallels here in civilian life.

Slamming his locker, Ben sank onto the hard wooden bench and rested his elbows on his knees. Soon as he gathered the strength, he'd change into his street clothes and head home.

Home. Well, that brought a chuckle. The studio apartment he shared with an empty fridge and a dead plant could hardly be called a home. He let his chin drop and cradled his head in his hands.

"Callahan?"

Ben lifted his head and slid the shift supervisor a sideways glance. "Yeah?"

The captain wore his uniform like a Brooks Brothers suit and never failed to comb his hair back with something slick and sweet smelling before he came on duty. Tonight he'd added a gold chain to his ensemble. Ben figured he either had a crush on the cleaning lady or himself; he wasn't sure which.

He pointed in Ben's direction. "Brody called in sick. I'm going to need you to stick around until I can find someone to take his shift."

"Aw, Cap. Come on." He rose to address his boss. "I'm beat. Send Fisher or Cappalini."

"Fisher's already left and Cappalini's wife went into

labor three hours ago." The captain shrugged. "That leaves you to ride along with Abrego. If it's any consolation, Vinson will probably jump at the chance for overtime. He's got those two kids in college now, and he's forever pestering me. Anyway, I left two messages."

Ben sank onto the bench. Even if he'd managed to gather the strength to protest, what would he say? All he could do was pray there would be no more calls before Vinson arrived.

Before he could fashion an official prayer, the radio crackled to life and another emergency call came in. He hit the rig running, then waited while Jerry Abrego slipped behind the wheel.

When Jerry called out the address, Ben froze. "Say that again." Of all the places to be called to, his exhaustion level aside, this one was the worst.

Jerry repeated the address.

Callahan & Callahan. Last time he left there, he swore to his father he'd never return. Four years, three months, and five days later, here he was, rolling toward it with lights flashing and sirens screaming. So much for getting in and out without his father seeing him.

Ben checked his watch. "It's a quarter to two in the morning. Are you sure this isn't a crank call? That's a department store."

Jerry shrugged and threw the vehicle into gear. "All I know is we got a call there's a dead woman inside the Cade's Point Boulevard window."

As the unit rolled toward its destination, Ben felt his heart begin to pound. *Get it together, Callahan. You've got a job to do.*

"You all right, Callahan?"

He cast a sideways glance at Jerry. "Yeah. Just tired, I guess."

"I heard you all blew out the old record last shift."

"Probably."

Ben scraped his fingers through his hair and focused on the road ahead. Two more turns and the building would come into view. He gripped the door handle and paced his breathing as they headed left on Riverside, then sped through the light at Wayland to turn onto Cade's Point Boulevard.

A police cruiser sat waiting, lights flashing. Jerry cut the siren and pulled up beside the officer.

"Over there." He pointed to the sole illuminated window, then gestured toward a man seated in the back of the cruiser. "That guy found her. Photographer. Seems as though he thought to get the scoop on these windows. Didn't expect to find a body when he looked inside that little tear in the paper."

"Male or female?" Jerry asked.

"Female," came the response.

While Jerry radioed the captain, Ben jumped out and grabbed his equipment before trotting toward the window. *Forget where you are, Callahan. This has nothing to do with Elias Callahan.*

"Anyone call the store manager?" he tossed over his shoulder.

"Not yet," the officer said. "Figured I'd wait until we knew what we had on our hands first."

"Probably could wait until morning at this point." The last person he needed to see tonight was his sister.

Ben shrugged off the last of his ire and leaned against the window at the spot the officer directed. Sure enough, a fair-haired woman lay prone beside what looked like a roaring fire. While he watched, her fingers twitched and she reached to rub her eyes.

"She's not dead!" he called as he tapped on the window. "I think she's sleeping!"

"Sleeping?" Jerry jogged up beside him. "Are you kidding?"

"Best I can tell through that little tear in the brown paper." Ben pointed to the spot. "Look for yourself, Jerry."

He did, then shook his head. "Don't that beat all?"

While Jerry went over to speak to the officer, Ben continued his efforts to awaken Sleeping Beauty. A moment later, the officer left with the newsman still seated in the back of the cruiser.

"Any luck?" Jerry asked.

"Not yet. What's the story with the guy in the cop car?"

Jerry shrugged. "I just got him for trespassing. Seems as though he was on the roof trying to shoot pictures through a skylight."

"Yeah, that'll get you in trouble every time."

"Especially at two in the morning." Jerry peered in at the woman. "How about I do the paperwork while you beat on the window some more?"

"I've got an idea." Ben nodded toward the unit. "How about you hit the siren a couple of times? I think that ought to do it."

When Jerry complied, the woman on the floor sat bolt upright. Ben tapped on the glass.

"Ma'am? City of Cade's Point EMT here! You need to come on out!"

She seemed bewildered and a bit lost. When he repeated his command, she rose and stood in the center of the window. Once more he tapped on the glass. This time she followed the sound.

A single eye peered back at him through the tear in the paper. It was blue—the color of a summer sky over the Pacific.

Ben took a step back, then tapped once more on the glass. "Come on out now! It's time to go home!"

She pulled the paper back at the corner and shook her head. Her lips moved but he couldn't quite make out what she said. Repeating his demand had the same effect.

He walked over to the trash can and yanked out a fast-food bag, tossing the contents back into the container. COME OUT OF THERE, he wrote on the bag, then walked back to the window to show it to the woman.

To his surprise, she lifted the corner of the paper to look out, then shook her head and disappeared. A moment later, she returned with a piece of what looked like a sales receipt. I CAN'T. THE DOOR IS LOCKED was written on the back of the receipt.

OPEN IT. YOU ARE THE ONE INSIDE.

The woman made a face as she wrote, then lifted the receipt into view. I CAN'T. I DON'T HAVE A KEY AND THE ALARM WILL GO OFF.

He responded with a quick, IT'S OKAY. THE POLICE ARE ALREADY HERE.

She shook her head. I WILL LOSE MY JOB IF MY BOSS FINDS OUT.

He gave this last claim a bit of thought. Alexis had the reputation of being a tough cookie, but would she fire someone for falling asleep on the job? Probably. She once gave away a puppy because it refused to come when she called. Then there was the episode with the peace-loving Chinese fighting fish.

Ben sighed then wrote, WHO ELSE HAS A KEY?

The woman turned the receipt over and scribbled, MR. RILEY.

Mr. Riley. Hal Riley. Ben smiled.

As a kid, he'd followed Hal all over Callahan & Callahan, and the old fellow never once complained or failed to answer any of his questions. The man must be well past retirement age by now.

GIVE ME A MINUTE AND I WILL GET YOU OUT.

Before she showed him what she wrote, she pointed to the glass. DO NOT BREAK THIS WINDOW.

Suppressing a chuckle, he gave her the thumbs-up sign.

She nodded and crumpled the receipt, then tossed it behind her. As he walked back to the rig, he couldn't help but wonder why he was going to so much trouble for a total stranger.

It didn't take him long to find Hal Riley's number; it was the same one he'd had for six decades. He answered as if he were sitting by the phone and said he'd be up at the store in under fifteen minutes.

Hal made it in ten, and despite the fact that he kept stopping to hug Ben, he found the proper key and fitted it into the side door nearest the window where Sleeping Beauty had been held prisoner.

"Thanks, Hal," Ben said once the door swung open.

The ancient security guard replied, "Anything for you, Bennie."

"No one's called me that in years."

"Well, now, I guess I should have called you Corporal Bennie." Mr. Riley looked him up and down. "Only it don't look like you're still on Uncle Sam's payroll."

"No, sir. I've been with the City of Cade's Point almost a year now."

"Well, how about that? Wonder why your daddy didn't mention that you were back in town."

Ignoring the question, Ben stepped inside. The familiar scent of designer suits, expensive perfume, and big money stopped him in his tracks. If Hal noticed Ben's discomfort, he had the kindness not to comment. Rather, the old man weaved his way through the darkened aisles with the expertise of a man who'd been clocking in at Callahan & Callahan since Eisenhower sat in the White House.

Ben, on the other hand, stumbled and picked his way through the maze, unable to match Hal's pace. He did fine, even at his slower pace, until he slammed his knee against the umbrella display.

"Want me to hit the lights, Bennie?" Hal called.

"No, don't do that. I'm fine." He wasn't, but somehow it seemed appropriate to be entering Callahan & Callahan in the dead of night under cover of darkness.

"Oh, there you are!" he heard a voice call. "You all just don't know how glad I am to see you."

Definitely not from around here, Ben decided from the way she drew out her words. Beautiful, he realized when he turned the corner and caught sight of her.

The woman came his way, right hand outstretched. Before he realized what happened, she was shaking his hand. Those eyes, much prettier when viewed without the glass between them, peered up at him with what looked like a mixture of gratitude and exhaustion.

"Casey. Casey Forrester. I don't know what I would have done without you, Officer."

"I'm not an officer." He withdrew his hand. "I just work for the city."

She studied his face for a second, then her attention

fell to his lapel. "Callahan." Her gaze met his, the exhaustion turned to amusement. "Same as the store. What are the odds?"

*Here we go.* How he hated having to explain away his connection to the Callahan fortune—or rather his lack of it.

"Yeah, what are the odds?" He caught Mr. Riley staring and gave the old man a wave. "Appreciate the help, Hal."

"Anytime," he said. "You take care."

Ben responded, then turned and headed for the door. Between his forced return to the store and the sleepy-eyed blond, he'd just made a memory he'd be hard pressed to forget. The sooner he got out of here, the better.

# Chapter 3

"Hey, hold on a minute, Officer Callahan!"

Casey picked up her pace to try and catch the long-legged fellow who'd just saved her budding career from ruin. Unfortunately, the man seemed more intent on getting out of the department store than in obliging her by slowing down.

"Wait," she called, "these are *not* my running heels!"

As soon as his broad shoulders cleared the front door, he whirled around to stare at her. She grabbed the door to keep from slamming into him.

"I told you I'm *not* an officer."

*And you're not very nice right now, either.* She upped her smile in the hopes his grim look might soften. It didn't. *All right. Plan B.*

"Sorry. The uniform confuses me. Back home, only cops and security guards wear that. But then the closest hospital's a 'fur piece,' as my granny always says."

Casey waited for the medic to smile. He didn't.

*Plan C.*

"Look, I just want you to know I'm really grateful to you for being my Prince Charming and rescuing me from the tower tonight. If anyone found out I was sleeping on the job, I'd probably be headed back to the Ozarks for Christmas."

Again she waited for some sort of smile, maybe even a glint of amusement in those ocean blue eyes. Again, nothing.

"Honestly, you saved me from a huge mess. Can't I repay you in some way? Maybe take you out for dough-nuts and coffee?"

"It's not necessary, really. That's my job, ma'am," he finally said without enthusiasm. "I'm no Prince Charming, but if you appreciate the service, call the city manager."

"I'll do that." She gave him a playful nudge. "Shall I mention you by name?"

The paramedic raked his hands through his surfer-style hair and sighed. "That won't be necessary. Just tell him it was Prince Charming."

"Oh, I'll do that, but I'll still make good on that

coffee and doughnuts. Just name the place."

Casey waited for the grin that would indicate he was teasing. It never came.

Without a Plan D, she shrugged and walked past the Callahan fellow. *Odd that a man who makes his living helping people would be so crabby.*

Stifling a yawn, Casey settled behind the wheel of her VW Bug and stabbed the key into the ignition. Maybe the Cade's Point paramedic was tired, too.

The car protested rather than started, a usual occurrence lately. Casey pulled out the key, counted to five, and replaced the key in the ignition.

Out of the corner of her eye, she saw the EMT approaching. Rolling down the window, she waved at the Callahan fellow. "It does this all the time," she said when he reached her window.

For the first time, she saw something besides aggravation on the man's face. He actually looked concerned. "You sure?"

Casey offered a genuine smile. "Positive."

She turned the key and prayed as the engine cranked to life on the third try. Someday she'd have to replace the only car she'd ever owned. In the meantime, she gave thanks that she had no car note to pay.

"All right then." He glanced over his shoulder,

then back at her. "Hey; you're welcome." The paramedic stuck his hand through the open window. "Ben Callahan."

Casey smiled and shook his hand. "Nice to meet you, Ben Callahan. I'm Casey Forrester."

"So you said." His gaze swept across her face. "Get some sleep, okay?"

What beautiful blue eyes. *Focus, Casey.* "I'm headed home."

His badge glinted silver under the streetlight as he took a step backward. "Would you like us to follow you to be sure you're all right?"

"No, I'm fine. Thank you, though."

He stayed a moment longer, then gave her a nod and turned to sprint toward the waiting vehicle. Before she could shift the Bug into drive, the paramedics had pulled onto Cade's Point Boulevard.

Casey slowed for the stoplight at Riverside and Cade's Point Boulevard. Up ahead she could see the vehicle signal to turn left, then disappear down Grant Drive.

"Well, that was an interesting night, Lord." As she crossed Grant Drive, she looked to her left and saw the ambulance off in the distance. "And an interesting man, too."

⁓

Exhaustion rolled over Ben like the waves at Cade's Beach, each one dragging him further toward the oblivion of sleep. Maybe he'd bunk upstairs tonight instead of going home. When he got this tired, any bed would do. Besides, he had too much to think about and not nearly enough functioning brain cells to do the thinking.

Stepping back into the world he swore he had left for good was enough to do any man in. Combine that with meeting a woman who'd literally taken his breath away, and he was a goner.

Ben closed his eyes. *Lord, what are You up to? I thought we had a deal.*

"Well, that was different."

He opened his eyes and glanced over at Jerry, then let out a long breath. "Yeah. Different."

"Who woulda thought our dead girl in the store window would turn out to be sleeping?" Jerry shook his head. "It takes all kinds. She was a cute thing, though."

"Yeah. Cute." Ben closed his eyes. When he opened them, Jerry had begun his turn into the station. A quick glance at the parking lot told him his replacement had not yet arrived.

"Hey, I'll do the paperwork on this one, then I'm

141

heading home." Jerry cut the engine and released his seat belt. "You go get some shut-eye. If the boss wants someone to roll out again tonight, he's gonna have to do it himself."

As tempting as that sounded, Ben wouldn't leave his post. Even if it hadn't officially been his shift any longer for several hours.

"I'm fine." He gestured toward the stairs. "Look, I'm going to find an empty bunk. Tell the boss if he needs me, call me, okay?"

"Yeah, whatever." Jerry pointed to the closed door of the supervisor's office. "I still say he can handle this himself. What is it with you? Don't you understand this is just a job?"

Despite his exhaustion, Ben smiled. "You really want me to answer that?"

Jerry nodded. "Sure."

"It's like this. If you knew someone really important— someone like the city manager or maybe the mayor, with the power to decide your future—was watching you work, wouldn't you do the best job you could for him?"

He palmed the keys and leaned against the front bumper. "Sure, who wouldn't?"

"Exactly. That's how it works with me and God. Even when no one else is watching, He is." Noting

Jerry's surprised expression, Ben shrugged. "I don't want to sound like I'm preaching or anything, but you asked."

"Anybody else said something like that to me and I'd be tempted to call it preaching. You?" He slapped Ben on the back. "You're the real deal. I'm glad you've got something to believe in."

*You could, too,* he wanted to say. Instead he smiled and parted company with a handshake and a quick, "Anytime you want to know more, I'm here."

As he lay in his bunk a short while later, Ben's thoughts drifted between what to say to Jerry next time he asked about the Lord and whether he should call to check up on Sleeping Beauty. The issue with Jerry was much more important than a slight infatuation with a blond Kate Hudson look-alike, and yet Ben knew that when the time came, the Lord would give him the right words to speak to the searching paramedic.

The blond? That was another story altogether.

Then there was the issue of his father. Ben rolled over and punched the skimpy pillow. Thanksgiving mornings in the past, he'd headed for the house in the canyon to be poked and prodded by maiden aunts who thought him too thin and teased by uncles who resented his firm stance on bachelorhood. Then came the big blow up with his father at the store.

Callahan males were a pigheaded bunch and Elias Callahan was the most pigheaded of them all. Ben's sisters would say Ben had inherited a good measure of that family trait, as well, but what did they know? He drifted off to sleep, wondering if even his mother, rest her soul, could have negotiated a truce in this ongoing war between father and son.

Probably not, as Ben refused to apologize for choosing to serve his country in the Marine Corps over serving his father's business interests at Callahan & Callahan.

Ben awoke from a dreamless sleep to the smell of something cooking. Lunch, he discovered a few minutes later when he slipped into his boots and headed downstairs. Passing on the turkey and dressing, he situated a slice of pumpkin pie on a paper plate and anchored it with a cover of foil. It sat beside him on the seat of his truck until the light at Mountainview and Riverside when a Channel 43 news truck ran the light and nearly broadsided him.

He pulled to the curb to scrape the pie off his floor mat with an out-of-date map of Los Angeles, then climbed from the truck and deposited the mess in a trash receptacle. So much for his Thanksgiving feast. Glancing up Riverside, he noticed what looked like a traffic jam at the next light.

"The big unveiling," he muttered as he jogged back to the truck and climbed inside. "Big deal."

At one time it *had* been a big deal. Being the sole male heir, Ben had done the honors at the annual post-parade Thanksgiving morning unveiling ever since he was out of diapers. Photos of Elias Callahan's future business partner went out on the wire services along with images of the store windows that never failed to draw a crowd. Afterward, at the traditional meal in the company dining room, he'd been given first chance at the turkey leg.

Ah, the perks of inheriting the keys to the kingdom.

Somewhere along the way, he'd lost interest and still he honored the tradition. Until four years ago.

Ben let out a long breath and shook his head. Easing onto Mountainview, he accelerated. Three blocks away a soft bed awaited, while up on Riverside a painful memory of what used to be was being filmed for the evening news.

The choice was simple. Why then, did he slip his cap on and hang a U-turn to head back toward Riverside?

# *Chapter 4*

"C asey, you do the honors." Elias Callahan leaned close. "And don't be nervous."

Don't be nervous? That was like saying don't breathe or don't blink. Oh, anyone could manage it for a moment or two, but any consideration of accomplishing it long-term was out of the question.

Casey glanced over at the store owner and he gave her what looked like an encouraging nod. As she raised her hand to press the giant candy-cane-colored button, cameras began to flash. She lost track of where the button had been placed. It took her two tries to make contact with the device, but when she managed, the music started and the curtains opened.

Through the spots dancing before her eyes, Casey

watched the crowd's astonished faces turn to smiles. Then the applause broke out.

She'd chosen to stand near her favorite window, the scene from Granny's house. Whether the other two windows were a hit or a flop was uncertain. But she knew from watching the crowd on the other side of the glass that this one had met with appreciation. Granny would be pleased.

Elias Callahan grasped her elbow and guided her away from the throng. "Miss Forrester, perhaps you would do the honors of posing in the window nearest the door."

Neon Noel. Not her favorite.

"Oh, I don't know, Father." Mrs. Montero gestured toward the replica of the Forrester family parlor. "I think I like this one."

A moment later, Casey stood in front of Granny's fireplace. A half dozen journalists awaited her upstairs, each having been selected to write about the new window dresser at Callahan & Callahan.

It was all too much, really, this attention. Coupled with her lack of sleep, the excitement made her woozy and she swayed. Catching herself on the mantel, she stared past the crowd on the other side of the window to the vehicles passing on Riverside.

A truck slowed and edged to the curb, its occupant's face hidden beneath a cap. He leaned against the steering wheel before turning to look her way.

Elias Callahan cleared his throat. "Miss Forrester, shall we?"

When she glanced in his direction, she saw he wore an odd expression. He, too, was staring at the man in the truck.

The look on the older man's face concerned her. "Someone you know, sir?"

Mr. Callahan turned his back on the window and headed for the exit. "Not anymore," he said, as he disappeared into the store.

The interviews lasted until midafternoon, then the group headed for Thanksgiving dinner in the employee dining room, an event that had begun years ago when the late Mrs. Callahan balked at serving Thanksgiving dinner after spending the morning at the unveiling. She'd elected to bring the feast to the store and a tradition was born.

By the time Casey left the store, she was sleepy, stuffed, and floating on air. Gary, the store's Web guy, had a stack of articles on the store printed out for her while Mrs. Montero advised her to go home and tape the news broadcasts. The clincher was when Granny

Forrester called Casey's cell phone to say she'd been contacted by a wire service for her opinion on the room that was supposed to be a replica of hers.

"How do they find these things out, Granny?" she asked as she snapped her seat belt and threw the Bug's gearshift into reverse.

"I don't know, honey, but don't worry. I told them it was the prettiest store window I'd ever seen. Well, actually. . ."

"What? Don't you like it? I tried hard to make it look just like your parlor."

"Oh, I like it fine enough, honey. I just don't understand why you'd want my plain-old house featured in a fancy store window. Now that beach room? That was a pretty one. Oh, and the window with the red snow? Well, I just loved it, even if I never would have dreamed up that color combination."

"I'm glad you liked it, Granny."

"I did, that's for sure. So did your mama and daddy. They'll be calling you next. I told them they had to wait until I had my turn since it was my house you used." She chuckled, then grew silent. "Casey, honey, I wonder if it's too soon to ask what day you'll be here next month."

"What day?"

"For Christmas. You *are* coming home for Christmas, aren't you?" She paused. "Why, the Forrester Christmas tradition wouldn't be the same without you here to be a part of it. All your cousins will be here. You've never missed a year, you know. None of you have."

Casey shifted into drive and headed the Bug across the parking lot. "Yes, of course I'm coming home. I wouldn't miss it. I just haven't had a moment to think about exactly what day."

"I understand. Just as long as you're here in time to have our special Christmas get-together with your cousins."

"I'll be there. I promise. I'll let you know the minute I make the plane reservations."

Signaling to turn onto Riverside, her phone beeped. A number she didn't recognize scrolled across the screen. Rather than cut short her call with Granny Forrester, she waited until she reached home to check her messages.

"Casey, this is Elias Callahan. I want to congratulate you on a job well done. I've been at this all my life and I've never seen a more enthusiastic reception to our store windows than I saw today."

She gulped and plopped onto the threadbare sofa. Elias Callahan was pleased with her work.

"I've left instructions with your supervisor that you're

to be given a week's paid vacation starting Monday morning. When you return from your well-earned sabbatical, we'll talk about a raise, eh?"

A week off *and* a raise. She gulped again. She'd only take it if it didn't affect her planned vacation over the Christmas holidays. Nothing could keep her from Pierce City at Christmas.

"Oh, and don't make plans for Christmas Eve. I'm hosting a dinner in your honor. The invitations went out this morning. How's that for a Thanksgiving surprise, Miss Forrester?"

❧

Ben stabbed at the last piece of pumpkin pie, then washed it down with milk straight from the carton. The football game ended and a commercial for a delivery company came on as he rose to head for the kitchen to toss his paper plate and fast-food wrappers into the trash.

While he tried to convince himself that somewhere in the Bible it said that a turkey sandwich eaten alone was preferable to a feast shared with a contentious parent, the nightly news theme song floated toward him. Without dishes to rattle or anything to clean, Ben followed the sound of the talking heads into the living area.

There, in living color, was the smiling face of Sleeping Beauty. The camera panned back a bit to show her standing in the window that resembled someone's living room—the window where he'd first seen her.

The window where he'd spied on her from a distance this morning. Now *that* had been a dumb move. Not only had he seen Sleeping Beauty, but he'd laid eyes on his father for the first time since he left the military.

Ben pushed the newspapers out of the way and perched on the edge of the coffee table. Snagging the remote from beneath yesterday's sports section, he hit the VOLUME button.

"The inspiration for that window came from my grandmother's home in Pierce City, Missouri," she said. "Every year my cousins and I get together for our traditional celebration before Christmas Day. Inevitably, it is snowing or has snowed, so that's a part of what I think of as Christmas. I call this window Dreaming of a White Christmas."

A reporter questioned her further but Ben heard none of it. Instead, he stared at the window designer's name, then reached for a pen and jotted it down in the margin of the comics' page.

Not that he intended to look her up. The last thing he needed was any connection to Callahan & Callahan.

Still, she *had* seemed nice and she *did* offer to thank him. That rarely happened in his line of work. Most folks weren't too worried about who was saving them, just that they were being saved. Some actually complained.

Maybe he'd let her buy him a cup of coffee.

A commercial came on and Ben hit the MUTE button as his phone rang. He groaned as he rose and padded toward the sound.

"Who would be calling me on Thanksgiving? Surely I'm not being summoned to work on my day off. Not again."

The phone rang a second time. He picked up without checking the caller ID.

"Look, I'm not coming in to work today, Cap. You're going to have to find someone else."

A click was followed in quick succession by the sound of a dial tone. Ben hung up and pressed the caller ID.

"Callahan & Callahan Fine Clothiers?" Ben took a step backward. "Who would be calling from there on Thanksgiving night? Casey Forrester, maybe?"

He smiled and punched the code for the call-return feature. As the phone rang, he ran over what he would say in his mind.

Unfortunately, he needn't have bothered. No one answered.

It was Friday morning, and Casey's shoe-box-sized apartment smelled like a florist's shop. Between the dozen red roses her mama and daddy sent her, the huge arrangement of blossoms from her boss, and the fragrant fruit basket from Mr. Callahan, she could barely breathe.

Slipping into her running shoes, Casey tucked her key into her pocket and headed outside for fresh air. Her walk to the beach turned into a run as soon as her shoes hit the sand.

What a glorious day. The sun rode above a light wisp of clouds and added just enough warmth to the morning to keep the stiff breeze from being chilly.

Casey vaulted over a clump of smelly seaweed, then picked up her pace. Mama told her this morning that back home in Pierce City, the streets were covered in a light dusting of fresh snow. It was hard to imagine that back home there were snowmen in the yards and fires in fireplaces while here in her new home there were people enjoying the beach and surfing.

She ran past Java Hut and headed toward the pier. A half-dozen fishermen sat in silence, their lines bobbing in the surf. Toward the horizon, she noted more sailboats than usual. Must be the holiday weekend, she decided, as she completed her lap on the pier and returned to the beach.

A half hour later, she landed on a stool at Java Hut's beachfront counter. The combination of Christmas music on the sound system and the beach on the other side of the counter made her smile. Only in California.

Someone had left the lifestyle section of today's *Times* on the counter, and she slid it over while she waited for her coffee.

"Sleeping Beauty?"

Casey turned to see a familiar face coming toward her on the sand. The EMT, her rescuer from two nights ago, only today in place of his uniform and medical bag he wore a wetsuit and carried a surfboard.

"Well, if it isn't Prince Charming. Hi, Ben."

He looked surprised. "You remembered my name."

"It's a gift. I remember everyone's name. Just don't ask me for directions." She stuck out her hand and shook his just as she heard her name being called. "Oh, my latte is ready. Can you stay a bit?"

Ben took a step backward and stuck the end of his surfboard in the sand. "Well, I don't know, I—"

Again, her name was called. "Hold that thought," she said as she jumped up to retrieve her latte. When she returned, Ben had leaned the board against the side of the building and come around to take a seat beside her.

Drops of water glistened in his short hair and dropped to his shoulders as he shook his head. The slightest hint of a sunburn touched high cheekbones and faded into the stubble along his jaw.

And then there were those eyes. Green? No, blue but with a band of deep gold around their centers.

*What am I thinking?*

Casey set the latte on the counter. "I'm sorry, Ben. I told you I would buy you a cup of coffee next time I saw you. And here you are. What would you like? Vanilla latte, maybe?" She pushed the steaming cup toward the EMT. "Here, you can have mine. I'll get another."

He eyed the coffee, then scooted it back in front of her. "Thanks, but I like my coffee a little less fancy."

"Without the vanilla?"

His smile was amazing. "Without anything but coffee in it."

She jumped to her feet. "One black coffee coming right up."

Before she could reach the counter, he caught up with her. "Let me."

Casey stood her ground. "No way, buddy. I promised

you coffee and doughnuts, and that's what you're getting." She glanced over her shoulder at the gentleman behind at the cash register. "A black coffee and two doughnuts for the officer."

"I'm not—"

"An officer." Casey grinned. "I know. I'm just teasing."

"And I'll pass on the doughnuts." He turned his attention back to Casey as he followed her to their seats, coffee in hand. "Thank you for the coffee. You didn't have to do that, you know."

She settled on her stool and watched the EMT find his spot beside her. "And you didn't have to save my bacon the other night. I really appreciated how you handled things. I was afraid I might have lost my job over what happened. I want you to know I've never fallen asleep on the job."

"I believe you." Ben lifted the coffee to his lips and blew on the steaming liquid before making eye contact with her. "So, what do you do when you're not sleeping in store windows? I mean, working at the store." He set the cup down and upped his smile. "See, I can tease, too."

Now that was an interesting statement. Casey gave her attention to the latte in her hands rather than meet his gaze. "Honestly, I haven't had much time to do anything else other than work since I've been in California. Well, I like to run. Does that count?"

"Sure."

"What about you, Ben?" She leaned on her elbow. "What do you like to do when you're not saving damsels in distress?"

Ben glanced at his wetsuit.

"Besides surf," she added.

"Knit."

She nearly choked on her latte. "Really?"

He chuckled. "No. There's nothing better than surfing. You should try it."

"I wouldn't know. The closest thing I've done to surfing is to try to sled down Jenson's Hill standing up." Casey giggled. "Trust me. That wasn't pretty."

# Chapter 5

"Why don't you let me teach you to surf, Casey? You're in shape. I'm sure you'd be great at it."

Ben tried not to groan as he went back to his coffee. There wasn't a thing about what he'd just said that hadn't come out sounding stupid. *You're in shape?* What kind of thing was that to say to a woman he barely knew?

Casey didn't seem to notice his embarrassment. "Honestly, I'd rather watch. I find it fascinating that someone can get on a board and ride a wave all the way to the beach without getting hurt."

"Oh, I don't know about that." Ben jerked up his sleeve and pointed to the pale crescent-shaped scar on the inside of his left wrist. "See that? Hawaii, five years ago." He turned his hand over and flexed his forearm, revealing the reminder of a run-in with a piece of coral. "Bali."

Casey grasped his right wrist and touched the back of his hand, tracing the network of scars that ran from wrist to elbow. "What happened here?"

Ben jerked his arm back and yanked on the wetsuit. "Afghanistan, three years ago."

"There's no beach in Afghanistan," she said with a slightly confused look.

"Exactly." *But there's a buddy of mine who never made it home.*

He shook off the thought and searched his mind for a change of subject. Thankfully the sound system did it for him.

"Oh, I love this song." She smiled and her face took on a faraway look. "It reminds me of home and snow and my family."

"Tell me about home, Casey."

For the next few minutes, his companion waxed poetic about life in the Missouri Ozarks, about a close-knit family that included three cousins who were like sisters to her. Ben listened and tried to imagine what that sort of life was like.

Sisters, he understood. He had four of them. But a family that let nothing come between them? Who were so close that their property literally adjoined one another? *That* he didn't quite have a handle on.

Too soon she finished her monologue and turned her baby blues his direction. "That's enough about me. Tell me about your family, Ben."

He swiveled on his stool and leaned his elbow on the counter. "Oh, you don't want to hear about that. It'd bore you, and it's such a beautiful day. How about we get out of here?"

She hesitated before nodding, then followed him around the counter and out onto the sand. Her Ole Miss sweatshirt and running shorts complemented her slender frame and fresh-scrubbed good looks, making her appear more like a teenager than a grown woman. She certainly was a fresh face among the usual California blonds he tended to date.

Not that he had dated anyone in a long time.

Ben reached for his board and hitched it up under his arm. "So, what would you like to do now? Looks like you've been running. I don't guess you'd be interested in a walk."

Casey placed her hand on his arm. "You know what I'd really like to do?"

"What?"

"Watch you surf." He must have looked as surprised as he felt because she quickly added, "Only if you want to, I mean."

"Yeah, sure, of course I want to." Ben paused to search her face for genuine interest. "Are you sure? I mean, I'll be the one having all the fun."

"I assure you," she said with a giggle, "watching will be much more fun for me than putting on a wetsuit and making a fool of myself."

"I don't know, Casey." He swept his gaze in her direction, then shamed himself for doing so. She was just so pretty, all the more so because she seemed to have no idea of her beauty. "I think you'd look much better in a wetsuit than I do."

"We'll never know, will we?" She tapped his arm, then pointed to the shack where beach chairs were rented. "I'll grab a chair and you go do whatever it is that surfers do."

"Um, Casey, we surf." Ben waved at the familiar face behind the counter at Jim's Surf Shack. "Hey there, Jim. A chair and a towel for the lady, please."

"A towel?"

"The wind gets cold down by the water, Casey."

Jim came around to give him a bear hug, then

grabbed a chair and towel. When Casey reached into her pocket, he waved her money away.

"It's on the house, little lady. Your boyfriend here saved my life. It's the least I can do."

"Cardiac arrest," Ben said by way of explanation as they crossed the sand to the water's edge. "And I didn't save his life. The doctors did that. I just kept his ticker going until he could get into surgery."

Casey accepted the towel and watched while he set the chair a few feet back from the water's edge. "Do you always do that?"

Ben looked up sharply. "Do what?"

"Refuse gratitude. Sometimes that's all a person has to give."

He opened his mouth but found he had no answer.

"Never mind." Casey settled into the chair and crossed her legs, then draped the towel over them. "Go ahead. Wow me."

"Wow me?" He grinned despite himself. "Is that a command, Sleeping Beauty?"

"It most certainly is, Prince Charming." She affected a bored pose. "To the waves with ye before I'm forced to nap."

Ben reached down to snap the safety line around his ankle, then straightened to see Casey's questioning look. "In case the board and I get separated."

A few minutes later, with the board beneath him and the rolling Pacific all around, he thought of her question about gratitude. Did he really do as she said?

True, he hated to be complimented, but with good reason. He'd fought the monster of pride most of his adult life. Born the nearest thing to a crown prince in a royal family that valued the male bloodline hadn't exactly equipped him for the life of humility the Lord called His people to.

Ben turned the board and waited for a good wave, searching the coastline until he found Casey Forrester. As if she sensed his gaze on her, she stood.

His ride wasn't particularly impressive, but Casey seemed to think it was. She laughed and clapped, then ducked away from the water he shook off as he approached.

"Again!" she called.

"You sound like my nephew."

"Oh, come on." She pointed to the water. "That was a little wave. I want to see you ride a big one."

"You do?" He gave her a sideways look. "What if I'm not that good?"

Casey dropped her towel onto the chair and planted her fists on her hips. "You're kidding, right?"

Ben's eyes narrowed. "I might be."

She swatted his shoulder. "Stop being so modest, Ben. Just once more, please?"

He knew she was right about his abilities. What he didn't know was how she'd figured him for an expert surfer.

This time it was a beauty, one of those perfect waves with just enough potential to warn the average surfer away. As always, the moment his feet hit the board everything went into slow motion.

Balance.

Speed.

Instinct.

Ben filled his lungs with salt air while adrenaline pumped a rhythm through his veins. He ducked under the curling water and rode the wave out until he could see daylight and Casey Forrester again.

As he floated to shore, he saw her. She feigned boredom, then giggled.

"Did I wow you?" he shouted.

"Oh, I suppose it was all right," she answered in a teasing tone. "*Wow* is such a strong word."

"All right. Watch this!"

Ben began to clown around, doing the handstand he'd perfected during his freshman year at UCLA.

Casey rose and pointed to a spot behind him.

At least that's how it looked from upside down.

He flipped back to a standing position and opened his mouth to speak. That's when the wall of water hit him.

## Chapter 6

Casey threw down the towel and raced for the spot where Ben went down. She barely felt the frigid water as it pounded against her legs and fought her progress.

One after another, the waves slammed her, but thankfully none were as large as the one that took Ben down. When the water reached a depth where she could no longer run, she dove in and began to swim.

Forcing her eyes open against the sting of the salt water, Casey kicked off her sneakers. Years of competitive swimming had not prepared her for this dip in the icy Pacific, and yet she couldn't turn back.

Ben was out there somewhere.

Something large and black caught her attention and

she prayed it wasn't a shark. Casey bobbed up to catch her breath and saw Ben's board floating in the distance. Unless the line snapped, Ben should be attached to the board.

Casey ducked back under the water and swam toward the black object. Another surfer reached Ben before she could and yanked him out of the water.

She surfaced in time to see the surfer drape an unconscious Ben facedown over his board. Blood trickled from a spot just above his right eyebrow and disappeared into a dark pool in the ocean. His lips moved as if trying to speak, but no sound emerged.

"You, there!" the surfer called. "Can you help me? We need to get him out of here before the sharks get a whiff of all this blood!"

Following the young man's directions, she climbed onto Ben's board and waited until he positioned his board beside her. With Ben's head and shoulders on one board and his legs on the other, they paddled at a maddeningly slow pace toward shore. Trying to speed up their progress only brought a warning.

Any faster, he asserted, and Ben would slip from the board.

Any slower, she retorted, and the tide would haul them back out in the opposite direction. By the time they reached shallow water, Casey felt like screaming.

The surfer eased Ben onto the sand, then stood back to address the knot of people gathered there. "Anyone know CPR?"

Casey turned Ben onto his back and put her training as a lifeguard at the YWCA into use. She'd repeated the process twice before she realized her patient was staring up at her.

"Hey there, Ben." She forced a tone of calm into her voice.

"Don't stop, Sleeping Beauty," he whispered. "You were just beginning to wow me."

❧

The next hour was the most humiliating of Ben's life. Thankfully it was Jerry Abrego who was on call. Any other EMT and he'd never hear the end of it.

Ben looked around and determined he was in the back of the rig, his back flat on the gurney. "You rolling alone, Jerry?" he managed.

"Yeah; they're still shorthanded. Funny thing is, the cap tried to get you on your cell. Now sit still and let me do my magic."

He grunted as Jerry began his work. "Where—is—she?"

Jerry nodded toward the front of the vehicle, then bandaged him up in silence.

"She—okay?"

Ben had no memory of how he got from the water to the beach, but he had no problem remembering awakening to find Casey leaning over him.

When Jerry finished, he gestured toward the glass separating the treatment area from the cab. "Your girlfriend?"

"Nah." Ben eased into a sitting position. "Just someone I—" He paused to let a wave of dizziness pass, then continued, "Met recently."

"You think I don't recognize her, buddy?" Jerry chuckled. "She's the dead woman from your daddy's store."

He shook off the dizziness and shrugged his shoulders to ease the tightness between them. The fog cleared and he could think again. His first thought was of the woman who'd rescued him.

"Yeah, about Casey. . ." Ben leveled Jerry a serious look and exhaled. "I'd appreciate it if you didn't mention anything to her about my connection to the store."

"You think she doesn't know?"

"Nah. She thinks the name's a coincidence. I didn't see any reason to correct her."

Jerry shrugged. "Suit yourself, buddy, but don't you think she's gonna figure it out eventually?"

Ben slid off the gurney and waited for his sense of balance to catch up. When the rig's back door came into focus, he psyched himself up and headed toward it.

"Ben, hey, where're you going?"

"I need to see how she is. You *did* check her out before you worked on me, didn't you?" Ben's feet hit the sand as he held tight to the door and then the bumper. The world tilted once, then righted. He heard Jerry follow a step behind.

"Yeah, I gave her a couple of blankets and turned on the heater in the cab. Told her to knock on the glass if she needed anything. Hey! Go slow, Ben!" Jerry called. "Come back here. You know the drill. You blacked out. I gotta take you in to check for trauma."

"Forget it, Jerry. I'm fine. The only trauma I've suffered is to my ego. I need to see Casey. I'm such an idiot. This is all my fault." He made his way around the rig to yank on the passenger door. "Casey? Are you okay?" She nodded but he didn't buy it. "Hey, Jerry, how about we take her in to get checked out?"

"No." Casey sat bolt upright. "I'm fine, really. I'm more worried about you. Are you okay?" She touched the bandage, and tears welled in her eyes. "I'm so sorry.

This is all my fault."

"I insist you see a doctor, Casey. You have no idea what damage hypothermia can do."

"Are you kidding me? I'm from Missouri where it actually gets *cold* in November." She fixed him with a stubborn glare. "I insist *you* see a doctor, Ben. You've had a head injury."

Jerry stood back, hands on his hips, and chuckled. "Yep. You're two of a kind, all right." He turned to look in Ben's direction. "You sure she's not your girlfriend?"

"Yes," they said in unison.

"All right then, kids," Jerry said, "how about I take you two home?"

While Jerry loaded Ben's board, Casey shifted over to allow Ben a spot up front. Her lips held a slight tinge of blue but otherwise she seemed to be unharmed.

"Hey, Casey, I was an idiot clowning around like that." He smoothed a strand of wet hair off her forehead while he checked her face for bruises. Under cursory examination, he decided she had suffered nothing worse than a swim in cold water without a wetsuit.

Truthfully, Ben was glad to have an excuse to sit, although he'd never let on to Jerry or Casey. When Jerry rolled the rig to a stop in front of Casey's apartment in the attic of a converted beach shack, he realized he only lived two blocks away from her.

"I'll walk it from here, Jerry," he said as he opened the door and climbed out.

"No you won't," Casey and Jerry said in unison.

Ben grinned. "She your girlfriend, Jerry?"

"Very funny," Casey said.

"Nice place you got here, Casey," Ben said.

"I'd hoped for a cottage on the beach with white roses and a balcony overlooking the water, but then I saw this."

"She's a regular comedian, Ben," Jerry said. "I say she's a keeper."

"On that note, I'll be saying good-bye and thank you to both of you."

Sliding over to the door, Casey let the blanket fall from her shoulders before climbing out. She'd walked halfway to the front steps before she turned abruptly. Ben stopped short to keep from slamming into her.

Casey took a step backward and studied her nails. "It's been an interesting day, Ben."

He touched the bandage, then turned the gesture into a salute. "I'm glad I could wow you, Sleeping Beauty."

"Oh, you did better than that, Ben." She lifted her bare foot to pointedly study her toes. "You knocked my socks off. My shoes, too."

"Yeah, about that. If you tell me what size you wear I'll replace them." Her lip began to tremble, giving evidence that the fair maiden was not yet over her distress, and he jumped into action by reaching for her elbow. "Let me help you."

"Are you kidding?" She stepped away from his grasp and took two steps up the stairs before she turned to chuckle. "I don't want to have to give you mouth-to-mouth again."

"Oh, I don't know about that, Casey. That was the best part of the whole day." Ben leaned on the stair rail and offered her the broadest grin he could manage under the circumstances. "In fact," he said slowly, "Miss Forrester, I can honestly say that you wowed me."

# Chapter 7

Casey's vacation wasn't starting off as the relaxing week she'd hoped. Rather, she spent the beginning of it wrapped in one of Mama's quilts with a box of tissues at her side. She'd missed church in favor of treating her fever and aches with chicken soup and hot tea.

By Monday afternoon, she'd exhausted her supply of tissues and moved on to paper towels. Her Jane Austen videos were groaning from overuse, and she had made short work of the pile of books she'd set aside to read in her spare time.

She'd made excellent progress in her sketches for the spring windows, even though the job had not yet been assigned to her. Still, memories of her day with

Ben Callahan intruded. He popped up in the books, the videos, and even the few TV shows she watched.

Every time a handsome man attempted to sweep a woman off her feet, Casey thought of Ben and his silly handstand. When a chaste kiss or the proper words of adoration turned the heroine to mush, she remembered Ben's parting words: "You wowed me." Even now they made her smile.

Then her cell phone rang.

She'd been careful to avoid calling Mama this weekend, choosing to e-mail instead. There was no need in causing her mother worry, and worry she would if Mama knew Casey was ill.

Casey leaned over the edge of her chair and fished for the phone beneath the magazines she'd collected on a brief foray to the corner grocery this morning. While she collected the phone, she also snagged another tissue.

"Casey, it's Ben."

"Ben?" She dropped her tissue into the overflowing trash can and sat up straight. "How did you get my number?"

A long pause.

"Ben?"

"You sound like you're sick."

Casey reached for another tissue and dabbed at her

nose. "It's nothing," she said.

Another pause. "Oh, man. I'm really sorry, Casey."

"I'm the one who should be sorry. My cold will be gone in a few days but you'll bear the scar of our day at the beach forever."

"Oh, I don't know. I worked half a shift last night, so when I got off I went to the early service at church. My sister was there and caught me with my bandage. Next thing I knew, she had me at the pharmacy buying stuff to get rid of the scar." He chuckled. "And here *I'm* supposed to be the medical professional."

"Yes, well, trust a woman to know about skin care." A thought occurred. "Say, do you go to church around here?" When he told her the name, she shook her head. "I can't believe it. That's where I go. You said you go to the late service?"

"When I'm not working a weekend shift, I do. You must be one of those who likes to get up early."

Casey shifted positions and burrowed into her nest of covers. "Now you know my secret. I'm a country girl at heart. Up with the chickens and sound asleep before the evening news. I figure that's why I'm not much of a sports fan. I never can stay awake to see who wins."

He laughed, then his voice returned to its serious tone. "Casey, I was wondering—that is, if you're not doing anything—well, of course, you're not because you're sick but. . ."

Casey gathered the quilt under her chin and tried not to smile. Was Prince Charming nervous about something? Could he be about to ask her out on—

"A date isn't out of the question, is it? I mean, if you're not feeling up to it, I'll understand."

It was her turn to be nervous. "When?"

"When? Well, I have four sisters, so I know I can't call you today and ask you out for tonight. How about tomorrow night? Seven?"

"You have *four* sisters?"

"Yes. Now answer the question."

"Tomorrow at seven." Casey pretended to think about it a moment. "I suppose I could do that," she said in the most casual tone she could manage.

Hanging up, she threw back her covers and jumped from the chair to do a happy dance. A moment later, the room began to spin and she fell back into her quilt.

"Slow, girl," she said as she reached for another tissue. "You've got twenty-four hours to make suffering from a cold look good."

❧

Ben dropped the phone onto the seat of his truck and

threw the vehicle into reverse. If he'd been home, he would have whooped for joy. Instead, he settled for a ridiculously broad smile and a trip to the florist.

"Callas and a white ribbon for Alex Montero," he said. "Just put 'Thanks for the number, sis. I'm seeing her tomorrow. Love, Ben' on the card."

Ben wrote his sister's home address on the card, then fished in his pocket for his cell phone so he could provide her number. Too late, he remembered he had left the phone in his truck.

"Is a number necessary? I don't remember Alex's home phone number and it's unlisted." He shrugged. "The convenience of cell phones. Sorry."

"What about an office number?" the florist asked.

"That I remember." After he gave the main number to Callahan & Callahan, he reached for a card from the counter. "I'll write this one myself." When he was done, he sealed the card inside the envelope and reached for the shopping bag at his feet. "I know this is nuts, but can you work these into an arrangement?"

"Sure. But this one won't go out until tomorrow."

❧

Between the prayer and the chicken soup, Casey's cold had been reduced to the occasional annoying sneeze.

She tucked a tissue into her purse and stuffed another in the pocket of her khakis, just in case.

Slipping her favorite blue sweater over her head, she reached for the brush and gave her hair a quick styling. When the doorbell rang, she dropped the brush and glanced over at the clock on her nightstand. Ben was early by half an hour.

She snagged the brush and tossed it onto her bed, then took a deep breath and let it out slowly. Heart racing, she walked to the door.

"This is silly." Casey reached for the handle and gave it a tug. "It's just a date. No big deal." The door swung open and Casey put on a smile despite her nerves.

Instead of finding Ben on her porch, there stood a young man wearing a T-shirt with FLOWER POWER emblazoned on it. "Miss Forrester?"

"Yes."

"Sorry this took so long. I thought I'd never find this place. I didn't even know this apartment was here." The man gave her a receipt to sign, then thrust an oversized bouquet of white roses in her direction. "Have a nice day, ma'am," he said over his shoulder as he raced down the stairs toward a green van.

Casey set the arrangement on her kitchen table and reached for the card. That's when she saw the shoes:

a tiny pair of white sneakers with pink laces attached to the soft pink bow. She removed the card from its envelope.

*Since I knocked your shoes off, I thought it only right to replace them. I hope you're feeling better. Forgive me?*

*Ben*

Smiling, Casey replaced the card in its envelope and set it beside the vase. She touched the toe of one of the shoes. "What an interesting man."

By the time Ben arrived, Casey had changed clothes two more times. When she answered the door, she'd donned a pair of black jeans and the green sweater her parents gave her for Christmas last year. This time she peered through the peephole first.

No great surprise. Ben looked fabulous. He'd traded his wetsuit for a pair of jeans and a navy sweater. The bandage over his eye had been replaced by a small strip of white tape, and the slight sunburn from Friday had faded to a burnished bronze.

"Hi," she said as she opened the door.

"Hi," he repeated.

"The flowers—they're beautiful. Just one problem."

Ben's grin sank. "What's wrong?"

Casey leaned against the door and pretended to study her nails. "Well, Ben, it's the shoes." She met his gaze. "They're too small."

## Chapter 8

Dinner was shrimp and crab, under the stars on the patio of a beachfront hole-in-the-wall in an enclave a few miles down the road. A lone guitarist played Spanish tunes while the Pacific kept rhythm. The ever-present wind died down to a gentle breeze by the time the coffee arrived.

Throughout dinner, the conversation had been about impersonal things like the mild temperatures last week, the headlines in the local paper, and the success of the fund-raising campaign at church. Casey had barely noticed any of these things, but listening to Ben talk made her smile.

Actually, everything about Ben made her smile. It also made her wonder what the Lord was up to.

Rather than dwell on the odd sensation that she'd never had a more wonderful evening, she leaned back in her chair and watched the waves break against the shore. "This is a lovely place, Ben." She turned her attention to her companion. "Thank you for bringing me here."

"My pleasure, Casey."

Casey took a sip of coffee and watched Ben order two pieces of the house special, Wow Cake, from the dessert cart. With a flourish, the dessert chef sliced two overlarge pieces of the flower-covered Italian cream cake and set them on the table.

"I guarantee this will be the best dessert you've ever had." Ben reached for his dessert fork. "My mother used to make this cake and, much as I loved her, she never made it this good."

Loved?

Several questions begged to be asked, chief among them what the current status was with his mother. Granny Forrester always said if a man didn't care about his mama, then run for the hills because he won't love you right, either.

She placed a small bite—just a nibble, actually—of cake onto her fork. When Ben made a face, she scooped up a bit more and added a touch of frosting before popping it into her mouth.

All she could say was, "Wow."

Ben nodded. "Hence the name."

Despite her good intentions, Casey ate the whole thing. After a refill of her coffee, she was ready to broach the topic of Ben Callahan's family life. What she couldn't quite figure was how to do it without sounding nosy.

She decided to start with his childhood. "So, Ben, did you grow up here in Cade's Point?"

He nodded. "Yep."

*So much for getting the man to talk about his past. Now what?*

"Ben, is that you? What happened to your eye?" a man asked.

A man in a dark suit and a well-dressed woman with upswept black hair and tiny, wire-rimmed glasses approached the table. Ben rose to embrace her, then shook hands with her companion. "Delia. Bob. Good to see you." He touched the tape over his wound. "Surfing accident."

"Looks like a nasty laceration, Ben," the man named Bob said. "I can take a look at that in the office tomorrow if you'd like."

"I'm fine, Bob. Honestly. Nothing to worry about. Say, where are my manners? Let me introduce you to my friend, Casey." He smiled in Casey's direction. "Casey Forrester, I would like you to meet my sister Delia Jenson and her husband, Dr. Bob Jenson. Delia's the eldest, so she's a bit bossy."

"And Ben's the baby of the family, so he assumes we all think he's adorable even when he's behaving badly."

Casey searched the older woman's face and noted eyes that matched Ben's, as well as a broad smile and twin dimples that marked her unmistakably as his sibling. Delia and Casey exchanged pleasantries while Bob spoke to Ben about the latest buzz at the hospital. Casey got the impression Ben did not see these folks on a regular basis.

Another warning bell went off.

The doctor studied her intently. "Casey Forrester. Why does that name seem so familiar? Are you in medicine?"

"Oh no," she said with a giggle. "I'm the new window dresser at Callahan & Callahan."

Bob and Delia whipped their attention toward Ben. "Isn't that interesting?" Delia said.

"Interesting indeed," Bob echoed.

"Tell me, Casey. How did you come to work at my fath—" Delia shook her head. "I mean at Callahan & Callahan?"

"Oh, that's quite a story. I graduated from Ole Miss in the spring with the goal of someday working at Callahan & Callahan, but in my mind it would be way in the future."

"Why that particular store?" Dr. Jenson asked.

"Promise you won't laugh?" When he agreed, she continued. "Ever since I was a little girl, I've dreamed of living in one of the store windows at Callahan & Callahan. They were just so beautiful."

Delia chuckled. "I assume you altered your goal a bit as you matured."

"Oh yes. Once I realized that what I loved about those windows was the creativity and the ability to transform a small space into a place where everything is good and happy, then I knew I was hooked."

"Hooked?" asked Dr. Jenson.

She felt the heat rise in her cheeks. "This is silly, really."

"Oh no, I'm interested," Ben said as the other two nodded.

"Well, I mean, it's not like I am a doctor or an EMT or a. . ." She turned to Delia.

"CEO of an international marketing firm."

Casey nodded. "Yes, or the CEO of an international marketing firm. I'm just a girl from the Ozarks."

"Casey, God can use anyone," Delia said, as she entwined her fingers with Ben's. "Absolutely anyone. Sometimes the less you know about His plan and purpose, the easier it is for Him to have His way."

"Yes, well, anyway," she said, "I believe the Lord put everybody on this earth for a different reason. Me, well, somewhere along the way I figured out He intended me to be someone He would use to add a little happiness to the world. Well, as much happiness as a store window can give, that is."

"I think a store window can bring an incredible amount of happiness. What do you say, Ben?" asked Delia.

Ben's gaze met Casey's and his smile broadened. "Yes, I'd say those windows have made a number of people happy. Just looking at them makes me smile."

"So you've seen them, little brother. Interesting." Delia fixed her attention on Ben. "So, Ben, we missed you at Thanksgiving. Were you working?"

The statement seemed harmless enough to Casey, but Ben's countenance darkened. "Yeah, you know how it is. The guy without the family draws all the holiday overtime."

Ben's sister placed her hand on his. "You have a family, Ben. Whether you choose to be a part of it is up to you. Don't ever forget that."

All the air seemed to go out of Ben as he looked down at his sister's hand. "It was good seeing you tonight, guys. We were just leaving or we'd invite you to coffee."

Delia went up on tiptoe to give Ben a kiss on the cheek, then Bob shook Ben's hand. When Delia stepped toward Casey, she paused. "Wait a minute. You didn't finish your story, Casey." At Casey's confused look, Delia explained. "You were going to tell us how you ended up at Callahan & Callahan."

"Oh, that. Well, all I can say is that it was a God thing. There's no other explanation. I was in my last semester at Ole Miss when I got the idea to send a résumé to Callahan & Callahan. It was a silly thing to do, because they weren't even interviewing on our campus but still, I felt God telling me to give it a shot. After all, it *was* my dream job."

She shrugged. "So I put a few of my sketches from design class in an envelope along with my résumé. I was about to write a cover letter when I realized I didn't know who to address it to. I called the main number for the store, not realizing I'd called an hour before the store opened. Would you believe the person who answered the phone was Mrs. Montero, the store manager?"

The trio didn't seem surprised by this. In fact, something akin to a knowing look passed between Ben's sister and her husband. Ben, however, looked positively pale.

"Mrs. Montero and I had a great conversation. Did you know she went to Ole Miss? Anyway, by the time I got off the phone I had an interview. Two weeks later, I had a job offer. I've been with the store since July. I don't know how to explain it except to say that God made it all possible because He's got some purpose in all of it. What that purpose is, I can't imagine."

Delia and Ben wore matching looks of stunned silence. Dr. Jenson took the lead and grasped Casey's hand. "I, for one, will pray that His purpose will become clear to you, Casey. And if I may say so, I may have an idea what that purpose is."

Ben's sister stepped forward and offered a smile. "Honey, I think this is between Casey and the Lord. I wouldn't advise you to spoil the surprise."

"Surprise?" She caught Ben's startled expression. "What's wrong, Ben?"

"Wrong?" He reached for his glass of water and downed half of the contents, then gave his brother-in-law the oddest look. "Oh, I don't know. Like my sister said, it's probably best that *the Lord* reveal things."

Bob seemed to think about the statement a moment before nodding in agreement. "Casey, it has been a delight meeting you. You have *no idea* how much I've enjoyed it."

Casey had the oddest sensation she was the only one in the group who was missing a piece of information. "My pleasure, Dr. Jenson," she said.

Delia stepped forward to embrace Casey, then held her at arm's length. "Take care of my brother. He's a pain but he's the only brother I have."

"Cool it, Dee," Ben said. "This is just our first date, okay?"

Ben's sister ignored her brother and broadened her smile. "As my husband said, it has been delightful. I will pray that the Lord reveals His purpose in your coming to Cade's Point very soon. In fact, Bob and I are having our annual Christmas get-together in a few weeks. I would love it if you'd come. May I send you an invitation?"

"Oh, thank you," she managed.

Delia nodded. "I'll call you for an address. Are you listed?"

"Actually, all I have is a cell phone. I'm never home so I figured I didn't need two phone numbers."

"Well, what if I just sent your invitation to you at

the store? That's probably the easiest way to handle things."

"Dee," Ben said, "could I have a word with you?" He didn't look happy.

"Well, of course, little brother. I would love to stay and chat but Bob and I were just leaving, weren't we, honey? Bob's got an early tee time tomorrow."

"Yeah, right." Ben wrapped Delia in a hug that lifted her into the air. When he set her feet back on the ground, he touched the tip of her nose. "Keep this where it belongs, dear sister, or I'll have to tell Pop the story of how Mom's favorite Faberge egg got cracked."

"Benjamin, you know that ugly egg got broken when you tried to throw my doll up the chimney, you little brat." She winked. "Besides, to tell Pop, you'd have to speak to him. So, in this instance, I would welcome being tattled on."

# Chapter 9

Pant legs rolled up and shoes in hand, Casey and Ben crossed the sand to walk toward the water's edge. With the waves breaking at low tide, the wet sand shimmered under the full moon.

They walked a few moments until Casey broke the silence. "What really happened back there, Ben?"

"Oh, you know, it's that brother and sister stuff."

He'd offered to take her for a stroll, as much to clear his head as to enjoy her company. Then there was the matter of the surprise he'd planned. The encounter with Delia and Bob had left him wondering if he ought to forget the plans he'd made for the end of the evening.

Casey looked up at him with eyes that shone in the

moonlight. His vague response had clearly not been sufficient.

"There was a weird vibe going on between you and the Jensons."

What were the odds that Delia and Bob would be dining at the Surfside Inn tonight? Worse, how had he managed to extricate himself and Casey from the encounter without his date knowing his secret?

Ben sighed. Eventually, he'd have to tell her.

A thought stopped him in his tracks. What if Delia went to Pop? By morning, Casey might be out of a job.

After all, if he were persona non grata at the store, anyone associated with him would most likely suffer the same status. What a shame. He was really beginning to like Casey Forrester. Telling her good-bye would not be easy.

He should do it now and avoid dragging out the inevitable. Yes, he'd speak his piece, tell her things between them were never meant to be, then go on about his business.

It was the only way to save Casey's job.

Once more, he looked down at Casey. Moonlight turned her face to a luminous pale, which served to accentuate her clean-scrubbed beauty.

Then she smiled.

Ben's heart sunk as his knees went weak. Oh, man, was he in trouble! All he could think about was how he could make this walk last forever. He'd tell her *afterward.*

*Lord, is that okay? Just one evening—then I'll break it off.*

Casey tugged on his hand and urged him to continue walking. When he caught up with her, he noticed she looked pensive. "Look, everything's fine, Casey. Don't let whatever's concerning you ruin a perfectly good evening, okay?"

For a moment he thought she might pursue the subject of Delia and the weird vibe. She surprised him when she took the conversation in an entirely different direction.

"Have you ever gone night fishing, Ben?"

Now this was a multifaceted woman. He guided her around a clump of seaweed, then steered her toward the rocks jutting out at the water's edge a few yards away.

"Night fishing? Yes, actually I have. Pop used to take me to the Cade's Point pier all the time. Why do you ask?"

She shrugged. "My daddy used to take me night fishing, too, and I wondered something."

"What's that?"

"Well, you know that look the fish has when it

breaks the surface? The one where he realizes he's out of the water and in for trouble?"

Ben chuckled. "Yeah, but I'm not sure where you're going with this, Casey."

They stopped at the edge of the small gulf between the rocks and the shore. Unwilling to commit to spending more time here, Ben prayed that the Lord would either lead him home or urge him to climb up to where a spectacular view of His light show would soon be had.

Casey touched Ben's sleeve and looked past him to the pounding surf. "Here's where I'm going with this, Ben: Back there at the restaurant before your sister showed up, you were doing just fine. I mean, we were having a good time, weren't we?"

He nodded.

"Then, here comes Delia and Bob, and pretty soon you were snagged up in something that made you look just like one of those fish. I just haven't figured out what that something was."

Ben closed his eyes and took a deep breath. He released it slowly with the intention of telling Casey everything. Instead, a soft whisper crossed his heart and he found other words.

"Casey, I can't explain this—I mean, it's crazy to say this, seeing as how we barely know one another, but I . . ."

She waited expectantly yet silently while he struggled to put together a meaningful sentence.

"What I'm saying is, there is so much you don't know about me, and yet I feel like I'm not able to tell you. I want to, believe me." He raked his hand through his hair, then touched the spot over his eye. "Every time I look in the mirror I'll think of you."

"Past tense." She looked down to study her hands. "Well, Ben, maybe it's time we head home. It's been a wonderful evening."

Out of the corner of his eye, Ben saw a streak of light followed in quick succession by two more. "Actually, if you'll bear with me, I did have one more thing planned."

Even as she nodded, she looked doubtful.

"How are your climbing skills?" He pointed to Outlook Rock, the centermost and tallest of the three formations. "Because we can either watch from down here or up there. Down here's not bad, but if you don't mind the hike, the view from up there is spectacular."

Casey smiled. "You forget. I was raised in the country. I was climbing trees while you were still playing dolls."

"Playing dolls?" He feigned indignation. "So, that's how it's going to be, is it? Let's see how you like California rock climbing."

Casey leaned against the smaller rock and dusted the sand off her feet, then donned her socks and sneakers. "Now I see why you told me to wear these shoes. I wondered when I saw the restaurant if I'd misunderstood."

"Follow me, little lady. You're about to see the show of your life. By the way, this is called Outlook Rock. We had the name before the software guy thought of it."

She giggled at his bad joke, then forged ahead. "One thing we don't have in Missouri is a coastline. I don't think I'll ever get tired of the smell of salt air and the feel of sand under my feet."

She'd just spoken his heart—odd how a girl from a landlocked state could feel the same as a man who'd been raised with swim fins and a wetsuit.

"Come on then," Ben said. "We don't want to be late for the opening act."

They traversed the maze of low-lying rocks, then reached Outlook Rock. "I'll go first and you stay right behind me. The trail's not steep, but there are a few spots that are a little tricky."

Five minutes later, they stood atop Outlook Rock. The view was spectacular in the daylight, with a panorama that included the mountains on one side and the sparkling Pacific on the other. On a clear day, you could see all the way to Catalina Island.

Ben pointed to a bag he'd stashed under a natural crevice this afternoon. He unzipped the duffel and pulled out a plaid stadium blanket. As he arranged the blanket, he smiled up at Casey. "Our box seats, milady." He pointed to a spot on the blanket. "You can lie there and I'll be over here. No funny business, I promise."

She didn't seem convinced. "Maybe this wasn't such a good idea."

"Remember, Sleeping Beauty, we are here to see the show. I'll put the duffel bag between us."

"Well, I suppose it will be all right." Casey took her spot on the blanket, leaning back to rest her hands beneath her head.

Ben settled beside her and leaned up on his elbows. "Even my sister will tell you I am a perfect gentleman."

Casey turned to look his direction. "So, what's the name of this show?"

"Just watch, Casey," he said. "It has no name—at least none that I know of."

As he spoke the words, another streak dashed from the heavens. Her smile warmed his heart. Until now, he'd watch a meteor shower over anything else. Now all he wanted to do was watch Casey Forrester.

Oh yeah, he had it bad. *Lord, what are You up to?*

"Did you see that?" Casey pointed straight up. "It

looks like God's throwing stars."

Ben chuckled and leaned back to see the meteors streak overhead. Occasionally, he succumbed to the temptation to turn his attention to the woman at his side.

Watching her watch the Lord's handiwork was the best show of all.

Casey said good-bye to Ben at the bottom of the stairs with a hug and a handshake, then nearly floated up to her door. What a wonderful evening. Sure, there were a few questions lingering in her mind about Ben, but her thoughts spun past them to remember more pleasant things. She'd seen starry nights and her share of falling stars back in Pierce City, but nothing as beautiful as tonight's spectacular display.

Ben had been the perfect gentleman, keeping to his promise to place the duffel bag between them. She'd stolen a few covert glances and even caught him looking her direction a few times. Still, he'd only offered a quick smile before turning his attention skyward.

Just as she closed the door, her cell phone rang. It was Ben.

"Did you lock the door?"

"Yes, I locked the door." She peeked out the curtains

to see Ben still sitting in his truck by the curb. Letting the fabric slide back into place, Casey leaned against the wall and smiled. "Why?"

"Just checking."

In the background she heard the *ding* of the ignition and the sound of the truck's engine roaring to life. "Well, thank you for checking."

"You're welcome. Casey?"

Casey took another look out the window. "Yes?"

"I have to go. I'm useless trying to drive and talk on the phone."

"At least you know that about yourself. Most don't."

Ben chuckled. "I don't want to hang up."

She watched the headlights come on. "You have to. I don't want you to risk getting a ticket."

"I suppose not." He paused. "May I call tomorrow?"

It was Casey's turn to laugh as she glanced up at the clock. "Ben, it *is* tomorrow."

"So it is. Well, then, how about I call you later today?"

# *Chapter 10*

Ben waited a respectable nine hours before phoning Casey. He caught her on her way out the door for a run, and, at Casey's insistence, he talked to her until she stopped for coffee at Java Hut. The topic: *It's a Wonderful Life* versus *Miracle on 34th Street*, the Natalie Wood version.

If he hadn't been on duty, Ben might have met her at the counter and took his turn paying. Instead, he settled for taking the rig out to gas it up and driving past to see if she was still there.

When he found himself circling the block to be sure he hadn't missed her, Ben realized he might be falling for the window dresser from Missouri. Funny how he didn't mind.

The rest of the week passed in a flurry of phone calls to and from Casey, all sandwiched in between runs in the ambulance. His day off was Friday, and they planned their second official date: a compromise from Ben's original idea of a surfing lesson, which Casey nixed. Instead, Ben borrowed Jerry's sailboat and conned Alexis's cook into preparing an impressive picnic lunch.

God blessed them with a beautiful day for a sail, and He added a fine wind for good measure. Casey learned quickly and soon took her turn at navigating the channel. Only the threat of missing lunch could coax her away from the wheel.

"Did you make all this?" Casey reached for a handful of grapes and added them to her plate of roasted chicken and Greek salad. "It's wonderful."

Ben carried his plate beside her. "It would be easy to take credit for this, but my sister's cook did the honors. Does it count that I thought of it?"

Her smile was glorious. "Yes, it counts. Now, tell me about these sisters of yours. You have four of them?"

The mention of his family usually froze his blood, but somehow he found he wanted to tell Casey about his sisters.

"Yes. Delia, whom you've met, is the oldest and

by far the bossiest. Alex comes next. She's the smart one. Then there's Alex's twin Andrea, who is five minutes younger and a world different. Alex calls her the domestic diva because Andi's goal in life is to make the perfect pot roast and never have a pillow unfluffed. She's the most like Mom. Finally, there's Jill. She's a nurse. Last I heard she was working out of a hut in Sudan providing medical care to war victims. Her husband is a missionary."

"What an interesting family. You must be proud of your sisters."

Ben nodded. "Yeah, the girls really are a quartet of unique women."

Casey set her plate aside and leaned against the cushions. "Do your parents have any grandchildren?"

"Seven." He popped a grape in his mouth, then swallowed. "Delia's got two, Alex one, and Andi had four at last count."

"What about Jill?"

Ben shrugged. "She says it's too dangerous to bring babies into the world where she and Kent live. I suppose it's all in God's hands, but I would like to see her with children of her own." He glanced at Casey and caught her staring. "What?"

"You like kids, don't you?"

"Yeah, they're great. Why?"

She turned to look in the direction of the wind, eyes closed, and her hair blew away from her face. "No reason," she finally said. "I'm just trying to figure out who you are."

"I'm just me."

Casey opened her eyes and regarded him with an odd look. "Just you? No deep, dark secrets?"

*Uh-oh. I don't like the tone of that.*

"W–w–what do you mean?"

She sat up straighter. "I mean, it surprises me that a man who knows so much about his sisters doesn't sit down with them on Thanksgiving."

He tried not to scowl. "I told you before. I had to work."

"Yes, you did, but I happen to know you got off early enough to stop in front of Callahan & Callahan and watch the windows being unveiled." Casey ran her hands through her hair and tilted her chin to meet the early afternoon sun. "But what you didn't tell me is why you don't talk about your parents."

*Time to change the subject. But how?*

He rose to yank at the rope holding the anchor. To his surprise, Casey came up behind him and put her hand atop his.

"I'm sorry, Ben," she said softly. "I don't mean to pry. You don't have to say another word if you don't want to."

Ben turned slowly. Casey stood close. Too close.

He sank onto the cushions and buried his head in his hand. *What now, Lord? Do I tell her?*

From somewhere deep inside, he felt the words well up. "My mother went home to Jesus when I was very young. I haven't spoken to my father since I enlisted." At her confused look, he continued. "Pop wanted me to go into the family business. I felt medicine calling me but knew I would never be able to afford med school with my father set against it. I settled for enlisting in the Marines. It seemed like a good way to get the training I wanted and get out of town at the same time. When I told him the news, he told me he no longer had a son."

Ben watched Casey take it all in, seemingly digesting the news fairly well.

"So, let me understand this. Your father was grooming you to take over his business but you became a Marine instead?"

"That's right."

"And because you chose the military, he broke off contact."

Ben shrugged. "That's about the size of it, except the breaking off contact thing was mutual."

He knew he'd answered all Casey's questions about his family when the topic turned away from the personal nature of his rift and toward the finer points of tacking against the wind. Glad for the interruption, he tutored Casey in the more difficult aspects of sailing until the sun began to sink toward the horizon. Too soon, he drove up to her house.

"I had a wonderful time," Casey said. "Thank you."

Ben smiled. "My pleasure."

Casey gestured toward the house. "I should go."

He released his seat belt and turned off the truck. "Let me walk you to the door this time." A statement, not a question.

When they reached the top of the stairs, Casey fished her keys from her purse. She seemed reluctant to unlock the door.

"Something wrong, Sleeping Beauty?"

She looked up at him with a concerned expression. "How old is your father?"

Ben did a quick calculation. "I'd say he's past eighty by now."

"I see." She touched her lips with her fingers, then sighed. "So, how long are you going to let this continue?

I mean, neither of you seem to be walking where God wants in the relationship, don't you think?"

Her question offended him. Then, it challenged him. Finally, it concerned him.

"I hadn't thought about it that way. Keeping this silence hasn't honored God, has it?"

Casey shook her head. "So what are you going to do about it?"

"Do?" Ben moved closer. "Well, Pop's not here right now."

"No, he's not." Casey smiled.

"And I have to work tonight, so going out to see him now is out of the question. So, what I thought I would do is. . ."—he leaned toward her—"is kiss you."

And he did.

Casey awoke on Saturday to a text message on her phone. MEET ME AT JAVA HUT ASAP. TEXT ME WITH TIME. B.

She slipped into her clothes and sent him a response. TEN MINUTES? C.

In no time, she received her answer. MAKE IT FIVE. I AM ALREADY THERE. B.

When she arrived, she found Ben at the cash register

purchasing a vanilla latte. "Good morning, Sleeping Beauty."

She accepted the coffee. "It is now," she said as she took a tiny sip.

He wore his uniform and a tired expression. "I wanted to thank you for yesterday," he said.

Casey felt herself blush. The kiss had been even more spectacular than the day. In fact, she had been reliving it this morning when he'd called.

"What do you mean?"

Ben raked his hands through his hair. "If I weren't so tired I'd go talk to Pop right now. See, you were right. I'm not honoring God with my behavior."

"Did I say that?" She took another sip of her latte. "It sounds kind of harsh now that I am hearing you say it."

"It was the truth, Casey." He paused and seemed to be studying the counter. "There's something else I need to tell you, and I don't think you're going to like it. See, my father is—"

His radio squawked to life. Once again, he was being summoned for overtime work. Jerry was running late and the captain needed a man to cover his shift until the EMT could arrive. He'd only be there an hour, no more, the captain promised.

Ben took Casey's hand and lifted it to touch his lips. "We need to finish this conversation. Can I come over tonight?"

Casey frowned. "I'm sorry, Ben. I made dinner plans with two ladies from work. I realized when I got stuck in the store that I needed to cultivate my friendships here." She paused to offer him a grin. "Just in case I need to call someone in the middle of the night and ask for help."

"Tomorrow after church then?"

"Sure. Now, come on. I'll walk you out." Casey rose and tossed her empty latte container into the trash bin.

He stopped in his tracks and shook his head. "I promised the guys in my men's group I'd have lunch with them. We're trying to decide on a Bible study. I'm on the evening shift, so I will have to go straight from my lunch to work."

"We'll figure something out, Ben," she said as they stopped beside the ambulance.

Ben looked to the right and then to the left before embracing Casey. He held her for a moment, then brushed her cheek with his lips. She looked up into his eyes and grinned.

"What a nice way to start the day."

"No, *this* is a nice way to start the day." He kissed her

quickly. "Casey, I don't know what's happening between us. Do you?"

*Yes, I know, Ben Callahan. It's crazy but I'm in love. Are you?*

# Chapter 11

Thanks for covering my rear, Ben." Jerry slipped behind the wheel of the rig and buckled his seat belt. They had a call, a nonemergency, and thankfully it came in just as his buddy arrived.

"I wanted to tell you why I was late."

"Yeah, okay," Ben said, "but you don't have to."

Jerry smiled. "See, I was all set to walk out the door when my kid comes in and starts asking me all these questions about God and stuff. Well, since you and I have been talking, I had some of the answers. The rest, we looked up."

Ben clapped his hand onto Jerry's shoulder and grinned. "That's great, Jerry."

"Yeah, and while we were looking up stuff, I found

that bookmark you gave me. The one that talks about how to ask Jesus into your heart." He paused and looked away, swiping at his eyes. "Well, um—the kid, he gets ahold of that bookmark and he says, 'Dad, you and me, we need to do this. We need to get right with Jesus.'" Jerry turned back toward Ben. "My boy's fourteen and he's got more sense than me. But now, thanks to you, we both got Jesus."

⧉

Casey found waking for work on Monday morning harder than she remembered. One week of languishing in bed and watching movies or talking to Ben on the phone had made her sadly inept at the work routine. To top it off, her in-box was overflowing with a week's worth of work. She would have to stay late to clear it out.

Ben called just as she sat down at her desk.

"Casey, we really need to get together tonight. It's important."

Casey cast a glance at the in-box pile that threatened to turn into an avalanche. "I can't see you tonight. I have to work. What about tomorrow?"

She heard him sigh. "No, I have to work."

The sound of Mrs. Montero's voice warned her of

her boss's presence in the hall. "I have to go. I'll call you at lunch." She clicked off the phone and stashed it in her desk drawer just as Mrs. Montero rounded the corner with another woman in tow.

"Welcome back, Casey. Meet my twin sister, Andi." She smiled. "Andi, this is Casey Forrester, the genius behind the Christmas windows."

"It's a pleasure, Casey." Andi reached across Casey's desk to shake her hand. "Alex has told me so much about you. Delia, too."

Mrs. Montero looked confused. "Delia?"

"I'll tell you all about it over coffee. It was nice meeting you, Casey. I hope to see you again soon."

Casey sat back in her chair and tried to make sense of what she'd just heard. Alex, Andi, and Delia. Where had she heard those names in conjunction with one another?

"Ben."

She rose on shaking legs and headed for the break room to fortify her brain with the store's signature French roast. Before she could pour her coffee, Mrs. Montero's secretary came in carrying an enormous arrangement of flowers.

"Those are lovely, Susan. Are they yours?"

"No, Mrs. Montero's brother sent them. The florist

made a mistake and delivered them here instead of her home last week. Guess this was the only number they had for her. Anyway, aren't they pretty?"

The phone rang across the hall at Susan's desk. "Oh, do you mind watching this until the water fills to the top?"

Casey eyed the card as she took hold of the slowly filling clear-glass vase that Susan had put under the tap. "Sure, I'll keep an eye on it," she said as Susan scurried away.

The envelope had been discarded, leaving only the card on the plastic holder. Casey parted the foliage in order to read the inscription.

> *Thanks for the number, sis. I'm seeing her tomorrow.*
>
> > *Love,*
> > *Ben*

"Thanks for the number? I'm seeing her tomorrow?" Casey's eyes narrowed. "And he let me believe the Callahan name was just a coincidence."

"Yes, I did, and I'm sorry."

"Ben! What are you doing at my office?" Casey dropped the arrangement and it crashed into the sink.

She looked at the mess, then back at Ben. It was all she could do to keep from crying.

"I came to see you." He shook his head. "Actually, I came to see my father first, then you."

Elias Callahan stepped off the elevator. "There you are. Oh, good, Casey, you're here, too. This is perfect."

Casey stared at Ben. "He's your father."

"Yes." Ben crossed the distance between them. "I wanted to tell you." He paused to capture her hand with his. "No, that's not true. I didn't want to tell you at all. Then you talked to me about God's will and I knew I had to." He gestured toward his father with his free hand. "I also knew I owed this man an apology."

Elias came to stand at Ben's side. It was obvious the man had been crying. "Casey, I owe you a huge debt of gratitude. You brought my son back to me. More important, what you said to him, he repeated to me. Those words brought me back to my son."

"There's more, Casey." Ben released her fingers to take her into an embrace. "I don't mind saying this in front of Pop. I love you. I can't explain it, and I know we haven't known one another a long time, but my prayers have told me that this has to be something God approves of."

Casey stood quiet a long time, struggling to find the words to respond.

"It's a lot to take in, Casey, but I know we were meant to be. Will you give us a chance?"

She tried to nod but couldn't. Finally she managed to speak. "I love you, too, Ben."

While Elias beamed his approval, Ben went down on one knee. "Casey Forrester, you are the world to me. Will you be my wife, Sleeping Beauty?"

This time Casey found her ability to nod. She also said, "Yes, Prince Charming, I will."

"This calls for a celebration. I know!" Elias clapped his hands. "We will turn Casey's Christmas Eve party into an engagement party for the two of you."

Casey's heart sank. "About that party. I've been trying to figure out how to tell you this, sir, but I can't be there Christmas Eve. I have plans to go home to Missouri. Granny Forrester and the family are expecting me."

Ben exchanged glances with his father. "What if I were to accompany you to Missouri, Casey? I want to speak to your father before I make our engagement official." He turned to Elias. "You understand, don't you, Pop?"

"Understand a man in love? Of course I do. What if we hold off on the party until Valentine's Day? We can plan the party to coincide with Casey's Valentine's Day windows."

"I got the Valentine's Day windows?" Casey jumped into Ben's arms and kissed him soundly. When he set her on her feet again, she realized she now stood in her bare feet.

"You did it again, Prince Charming," she said as she looked up into the eyes of the man she loved.

"What did I do, Sleeping Beauty?"

"You knocked my socks off. Well, my shoes, anyway."

## KATHLEEN MILLER

A publicist for Glass Road Public Relations, Kathleen is a tenth-generation Texan and mother of three grown sons and a teenage daughter. She is a graduate of Texas A&M University and an award-winning novelist of Christian fiction whose first published work jumped onto the Christian Booksellers Association best-seller list in its first month of release. Kathleen is a former treasurer for the American Christian Fiction Writers and is a member of Inspirational Writers Alive, Romance Writers of America, Words for the Journey Christian Writers Guild, Fellowship of Christian Writers, and The Writers Guild. In addition, she speaks on the craft of writing to schools and writing groups and teaches an online creative writing course through Lamar University in Beaumont, Texas.

# A Letter to Our Readers

Dear Readers:

In order that we might better contribute to your reading enjoyment, we would appreciate your taking a few minutes to respond to the following questions. When completed, please return to the following: Fiction Editor, Barbour Publishing, Inc., P.O. Box 719, Uhrichsville, OH 44683.

1. Did you enjoy reading *Mountains, Memories & Mistletoe*?
   ❏ Very much—I would like to see more books like this.
   ❏ Moderately—I would have enjoyed it more if _____
   _____
   _____

2. What influenced your decision to purchase this book?
   (Check those that apply.)
   ❏ Cover          ❏ Back cover copy      ❏ Title       ❏ Price
   ❏ Friends        ❏ Publicity            ❏ Other

3. Which story was your favorite?
   ❏ *Making Memories*
   ❏ *Dreaming of a White Christmas*

4. Please check your age range:
   ❏ Under 18       ❏ 18–24                ❏ 25–34
   ❏ 35–45          ❏ 46–55                ❏ Over 55

5. How many hours per week do you read? _____

Name _____

Occupation _____

Address _____

City_____ State _____ Zip_____

E-mail_____